J. M. Coetzee

DISGRACE

VINTAGE

Published by Vintage 2000

38

Copyright © J. M. Coetzee 1999

First published in Great Britain in 1999
by Martin Secker & Warburg

Vintage Books
Random House, 20 Vauxhall Bridge Road,
London SW1V 2SA

www.vintage-books.co.uk

Addresses for companies within The Random House Group Limited
can be found at: www.randomhouse.co.uk/offices.htm

The Random House Group Limited Reg. No. 954009

A CIP catalogue record for this book
is available from the British Library

ISBN 9780099284826

Penguin Random House is committed to a sustainable future for
our business, our readers and our planet. This book is made from
Forest Stewardship Council® certified paper.

Printed and bound in Great Britain by Clays Ltd, St Ives plc

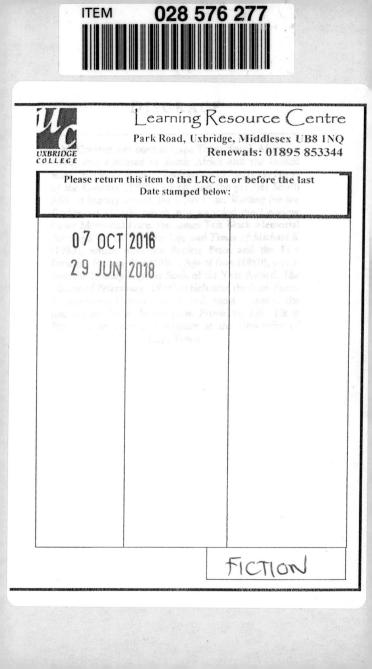

ONE

FOR A MAN of his age, fifty-two, divorced, he has, to his mind, solved the problem of sex rather well. On Thursday afternoons he drives to Green Point. Punctually at two p.m. he presses the buzzer at the entrance to Windsor Mansions, speaks his name, and enters. Waiting for him at the door of No. 113 is Soraya. He goes straight through to the bedroom, which is pleasant-smelling and softly lit, and undresses. Soraya emerges from the bathroom, drops her robe, slides into bed beside him. 'Have you missed me?' she asks. 'I miss you all the time,' he replies. He strokes her honey-brown body, unmarked by the sun; he stretches her out, kisses her breasts; they make love.

Soraya is tall and slim, with long black hair and dark, liquid eyes. Technically he is old enough to be her father; but then, technically, one can be a father at twelve. He has been on her books for over a year; he finds her entirely satisfactory. In the desert of the week Thursday has become an oasis of *luxe et volupté*.

In bed Soraya is not effusive. Her temperament is in fact rather quiet, quiet and docile. In her general opinions she is surprisingly moralistic. She is offended by tourists who bare their breasts ('udders', she calls them) on public beaches; she thinks vagabonds should be rounded up and put to work sweeping the streets. How she reconciles her opinions with her line of business he does not ask.

1

Because he takes pleasure in her, because his pleasure is unfailing, an affection has grown up in him for her. To some degree, he believes, this affection is reciprocated. Affection may not be love, but it is at least its cousin. Given their unpromising beginnings, they have been lucky, the two of them: he to have found her, she to have found him.

His sentiments are, he is aware, complacent, even uxorious. Nevertheless he does not cease to hold to them.

For a ninety-minute session he pays her R400, of which half goes to Discreet Escorts. It seems a pity that Discreet Escorts should get so much. But they own No. 113 and other flats in Windsor Mansions; in a sense they own Soraya too, this part of her, this function.

He has toyed with the idea of asking her to see him in her own time. He would like to spend an evening with her, perhaps even a whole night. But not the morning after. He knows too much about himself to subject her to a morning after, when he will be cold, surly, impatient to be alone.

That is his temperament. His temperament is not going to change, he is too old for that. His temperament is fixed, set. The skull, followed by the temperament: the two hardest parts of the body.

Follow your temperament. It is not a philosophy, he would not dignify it with that name. It is a rule, like the Rule of St Benedict.

He is in good health, his mind is clear. By profession he is, or has been, a scholar, and scholarship still engages, intermittently, the core of him. He lives within his income, within his temperament, within his emotional means. Is he happy? By most measurements, yes, he believes he is. However, he has not forgotten the last chorus of *Oedipus*: Call no man happy until he is dead.

In the field of sex his temperament, though intense, has never been passionate. Were he to choose a totem, it would be the snake. Intercourse between Soraya and himself must be, he imagines, rather like the copulation of snakes: lengthy, absorbed, but rather abstract, rather dry, even at its hottest.

Is Soraya's totem the snake too? No doubt with other men she becomes another woman: *la donna è mobile*. Yet at the level of temperament her affinity with him can surely not be feigned.

Though by occupation she is a loose woman he trusts her, within limits. During their sessions he speaks to her with a certain freedom, even on occasion unburdens himself. She knows the facts of his life. She has heard the stories of his two marriages, knows about his daughter and his daughter's ups and downs. She knows many of his opinions.

Of her life outside Windsor Mansions Soraya reveals nothing. Soraya is not her real name, that he is sure of. There are signs she has borne a child, or children. It may be that she is not a professional at all. She may work for the agency only one or two afternoons a week, and for the rest live a respectable life in the suburbs, in Rylands or Athlone. That would be unusual for a Muslim, but all things are possible these days.

About his own job he says little, not wanting to bore her. He earns his living at the Cape Technical University, formerly Cape Town University College. Once a professor of modern languages, he has been, since Classics and Modern Languages were closed down as part of the great rationalization, adjunct professor of communications. Like all rationalized personnel, he is allowed to offer one special-field course a year, irrespective of enrolment, because that is good for morale. This year he is offering a course in the Romantic poets. For the rest he teaches Communications 101, 'Communication Skills', and Communications 201, 'Advanced Communication Skills'.

Although he devotes hours of each day to his new discipline, he finds its first premise, as enunciated in the Communications 101 handbook, preposterous: 'Human society has created language in order that we may communicate our thoughts, feelings and intentions to each other.' His own opinion, which he does not air, is that the origins of speech lie in song, and the origins of song in the need to fill out with sound the overlarge and rather empty human soul.

In the course of a career stretching back a quarter of a century he has published three books, none of which has caused a stir or even a ripple: the first on opera (*Boito and the Faust Legend: The Genesis of Mefistofele*), the second on vision as eros (*The Vision of Richard of St Victor*), the third on Wordsworth and history (*Wordsworth and the Burden of the Past*).

In the past few years he has been playing with the idea of a work on Byron. At first he had thought it would be another book, another critical opus. But all his sallies at writing it have bogged down in tedium. The truth is, he is tired of criticism, tired of prose measured by the yard. What he wants to write is music: *Byron in Italy*, a meditation on love between the sexes in the form of a chamber opera.

Through his mind, while he faces his Communications classes, flit phrases, tunes, fragments of song from the unwritten work. He has never been much of a teacher; in this transformed and, to his mind, emasculated institution of learning he is more out of place than ever. But then, so are other of his colleagues from the old days, burdened with upbringings inappropriate to the tasks they are set to perform; clerks in a post-religious age.

Because he has no respect for the material he teaches, he makes no impression on his students. They look through him when he speaks, forget his name. Their indifference galls him more than he will admit. Nevertheless he fulfils to the letter his obligations toward them, their parents, and the state. Month after month he sets, collects, reads, and annotates their assignments, correcting lapses in punctuation, spelling and usage, interrogating weak

4

arguments, appending to each paper a brief, considered critique.

He continues to teach because it provides him with a livelihood; also because it teaches him humility, brings it home to him who he is in the world. The irony does not escape him: that the one who comes to teach learns the keenest of lessons, while those who come to learn learn nothing. It is a feature of his profession on which he does not remark to Soraya. He doubts there is an irony to match it in hers.

In the kitchen of the flat in Green Point there are a kettle, plastic cups, a jar of instant coffee, a bowl with sachets of sugar. The refrigerator holds a supply of bottled water. In the bathroom there is soap and a pile of towels, in the cupboard clean bedlinen. Soraya keeps her makeup in an overnight bag. A place of assignation, nothing more, functional, clean, well regulated.

The first time Soraya received him she wore vermilion lipstick and heavy eyeshadow. Not liking the stickiness of the makeup, he asked her to wipe it off. She obeyed, and has never worn it since. A ready learner, compliant, pliant.

He likes giving her presents. At New Year he gave her an enamelled bracelet, at Eid a little malachite heron that caught his eye in a curio shop. He enjoys her pleasure, which is quite unaffected.

It surprises him that ninety minutes a week of a woman's company are enough to make him happy, who used to think he needed a wife, a home, a marriage. His needs turn out to be quite light, after all, light and fleeting, like those of a butterfly. No emotion, or none but the deepest, the most unguessed-at: a ground bass of contentedness, like the hum of traffic that lulls the city-dweller to sleep, or like the silence of the night to countryfolk.

He thinks of Emma Bovary, coming home sated, glazen-eyed, from an afternoon of reckless fucking. *So this is bliss!*, says Emma,

5

marvelling at herself in the mirror. *So this is the bliss the poets speak of!* Well, if poor ghostly Emma were ever to find her way to Cape Town, he would bring her along one Thursday afternoon to show her what bliss can be: a moderate bliss, a moderated bliss.

Then one Saturday morning everything changes. He is in the city on business; he is walking down St George's Street when his eyes fall on a slim figure ahead of him in the crowd. It is Soraya, unmistakably, flanked by two children, two boys. They are carrying parcels; they have been shopping.

He hesitates, then follows at a distance. They disappear into Captain Dorego's Fish Inn. The boys have Soraya's lustrous hair and dark eyes. They can only be her sons.

He walks on, turns back, passes Captain Dorego's a second time. The three are seated at a table in the window. For an instant, through the glass, Soraya's eyes meet his.

He has always been a man of the city, at home amid a flux of bodies where eros stalks and glances flash like arrows. But this glance between himself and Soraya he regrets at once.

At their rendezvous the next Thursday neither mentions the incident. Nonetheless, the memory hangs uneasily over them. He has no wish to upset what must be, for Soraya, a precarious double life. He is all for double lives, triple lives, lives lived in compartments. Indeed, he feels, if anything, greater tenderness for her. *Your secret is safe with me*, he would like to say.

But neither he nor she can put aside what has happened. The two little boys become presences between them, playing quiet as shadows in a corner of the room where their mother and the strange man couple. In Soraya's arms he becomes, fleetingly, their father: foster-father, step-father, shadow-father. Leaving her bed afterwards, he feels their eyes flicker over him covertly, curiously.

His thoughts turn, despite himself, to the other father, the real one. Does he have any inkling of what his wife is up to, or has he elected the bliss of ignorance?

He himself has no son. His childhood was spent in a family of women. As mother, aunts, sisters fell away, they were replaced in due course by mistresses, wives, a daughter. The company of women made of him a lover of women and, to an extent, a womanizer. With his height, his good bones, his olive skin, his flowing hair, he could always count on a degree of magnetism. If he looked at a woman in a certain way, with a certain intent, she would return his look, he could rely on that. That was how he lived; for years, for decades, that was the backbone of his life.

Then one day it all ended. Without warning his powers fled. Glances that would once have responded to his slid over, past, through him. Overnight he became a ghost. If he wanted a woman he had to learn to pursue her; often, in one way or another, to buy her.

He existed in an anxious flurry of promiscuity. He had affairs with the wives of colleagues; he picked up tourists in bars on the waterfront or at the Club Italia; he slept with whores.

His introduction to Soraya took place in a dim little sitting-room off the front office of Discreet Escorts, with Venetian blinds over the windows, pot plants in the corners, stale smoke hanging in the air. She was on their books under 'Exotic'. The photograph showed her with a red passion-flower in her hair and the faintest of lines at the corners of her eyes. The entry said 'Afternoons only'. That was what decided him: the promise of shuttered rooms, cool sheets, stolen hours.

From the beginning it was satisfactory, just what he wanted. A bull's eye. In a year he has not needed to go back to the agency.

Then the accident in St George's Street, and the strangeness that has followed. Though Soraya still keeps her appointments, he feels a growing coolness as she transforms herself into just another woman and him into just another client.

7

He has a shrewd idea of how prostitutes speak among themselves about the men who frequent them, the older men in particular. They tell stories, they laugh, but they shudder too, as one shudders at a cockroach in a washbasin in the middle of the night. Soon, daintily, maliciously, he will be shuddered over. It is a fate he cannot escape.

On the fourth Thursday after the incident, as he is leaving the apartment, Soraya makes the announcement he has been steeling himself against. 'My mother is ill. I'm going to take a break to look after her. I won't be here next week.'

'Will I see you the week after?'

'I'm not sure. It depends on how she gets on. You had better phone first.'

'I don't have a number.'

'Phone the agency. They'll know.'

He waits a few days, then telephones the agency. Soraya? Soraya has left us, says the man. No, we cannot put you in touch with her, that would be against house rules. Would you like an introduction to another of our hostesses? Lots of exotics to choose from – Malaysian, Thai, Chinese, you name it.

He spends an evening with another Soraya – Soraya has become, it seems, a popular *nom de commerce* – in a hotel room in Long Street. This one is no more than eighteen, unpractised, to his mind coarse. 'So what do you do?' she says as she slips off her clothes. 'Export-import,' he says. 'You don't say,' she says.

There is a new secretary in his department. He takes her to lunch at a restaurant a discreet distance from the campus and listens while, over shrimp salad, she complains about her sons' school. Drug-pedlars hang around the playing-fields, she says, and the police do nothing. For the past three years she and her husband have had their name on a list at the New Zealand consulate, to emigrate. 'You people had it easier. I mean,

8

whatever the rights and wrongs of the situation, at least you knew where you were.'

'You people?' he says. 'What people?'

'I mean your generation. Now people just pick and choose which laws they want to obey. It's anarchy. How can you bring up children when there's anarchy all around?'

Her name is Dawn. The second time he takes her out they stop at his house and have sex. It is a failure. Bucking and clawing, she works herself into a froth of excitement that in the end only repels him. He lends her a comb, drives her back to the campus.

After that he avoids her, taking care to skirt the office where she works. In return she gives him a hurt look, then snubs him.

He ought to give up, retire from the game. At what age, he wonders, did Origen castrate himself? Not the most graceful of solutions, but then ageing is not a graceful business. A clearing of the decks, at least, so that one can turn one's mind to the proper business of the old: preparing to die.

Might one approach a doctor and ask for it? A simple enough operation, surely: they do it to animals every day, and animals survive well enough, if one ignores a certain residue of sadness. Severing, tying off: with local anaesthetic and a steady hand and a modicum of phlegm one might even do it oneself, out of a textbook. A man on a chair snipping away at himself: an ugly sight, but no more ugly, from a certain point of view, than the same man exercising himself on the body of a woman.

There is still Soraya. He ought to close that chapter. Instead, he pays a detective agency to track her down. Within days he has her real name, her address, her telephone number. He telephones at nine in the morning, when the husband and children will be out. 'Soraya?' he says. 'This is David. How are you? When can I see you again?'

A long silence before she speaks. 'I don't know who you are,'

9

she says. 'You are harassing me in my own house. I demand you will never phone me here again, never.'

Demand. She means *command*. Her shrillness surprises him: there has been no intimation of it before. But then, what should a predator expect when he intrudes into the vixen's nest, into the home of her cubs?

He puts down the telephone. A shadow of envy passes over him for the husband he has never seen.

TWO

WITHOUT THE Thursday interludes the week is as featureless as a desert. There are days when he does not know what to do with himself.

He spends more time in the university library, reading all he can find on the wider Byron circle, adding to notes that already fill two fat files. He enjoys the late-afternoon quiet of the reading room, enjoys the walk home afterwards: the brisk winter air, the damp, gleaming streets.

He is returning home one Friday evening, taking the long route through the old college gardens, when he notices one of his students on the path ahead of him. Her name is Melanie Isaacs, from his Romantics course. Not the best student but not the worst either: clever enough, but unengaged.

She is dawdling; he soon catches up with her. 'Hello,' he says.

She smiles back, bobbing her head, her smile sly rather than shy. She is small and thin, with close-cropped black hair, wide, almost Chinese cheekbones, large, dark eyes. Her outfits are always striking. Today she wears a maroon miniskirt with a mustard-coloured sweater and black tights; the gold baubles on her belt match the gold balls of her earrings.

He is mildly smitten with her. It is no great matter: barely a term passes when he does not fall for one or other of his charges. Cape Town: a city prodigal of beauty, of beauties.

Does she know he has an eye on her? Probably. Women are sensitive to it, to the weight of the desiring gaze.

It has been raining; from the pathside runnels comes the soft rush of water.

'My favourite season, my favourite time of day,' he remarks. 'Do you live around here?'

'Across the line. I share a flat.'

'Is Cape Town your home?'

'No, I grew up in George.'

'I live just nearby. Can I invite you in for a drink?'

A pause, cautious. 'OK. But I have to be back by seven-thirty.'

From the gardens they pass into the quiet residential pocket where he has lived for the past twelve years, first with Rosalind, then, after the divorce, alone.

He unlocks the security gate, unlocks the door, ushers the girl in. He switches on lights, takes her bag. There are raindrops on her hair. He stares, frankly ravished. She lowers her eyes, offering the same evasive and perhaps even coquettish little smile as before.

In the kitchen he opens a bottle of Meerlust and sets out biscuits and cheese. When he returns she is standing at the bookshelves, head on one side, reading titles. He puts on music: the Mozart clarinet quintet.

Wine, music: a ritual that men and women play out with each other. Nothing wrong with rituals, they were invented to ease the awkward passages. But the girl he has brought home is not just thirty years his junior: she is a student, his student, under his tutelage. No matter what passes between them now, they will have to meet again as teacher and pupil. Is he prepared for that?

'Are you enjoying the course?' he asks.

'I liked Blake. I liked the Wonderhorn stuff.'

'Wunderhorn.'

'I'm not so crazy about Wordsworth.'

'You shouldn't be saying that to me. Wordsworth has been one of my masters.'

It is true. For as long as he can remember, the harmonies of *The Prelude* have echoed within him.

'Maybe by the end of the course I'll appreciate him more. Maybe he'll grow on me.'

'Maybe. But in my experience poetry speaks to you either at first sight or not at all. A flash of revelation and a flash of response. Like lightning. Like falling in love.'

Like falling in love. Do the young still fall in love, or is that mechanism obsolete by now, unnecessary, quaint, like steam locomotion? He is out of touch, out of date. Falling in love could have fallen out of fashion and come back again half a dozen times, for all he knows.

'Do you write poetry yourself?' he asks.

'I did when I was at school. I wasn't very good. I haven't got the time now.'

'And passions? Do you have any literary passions?'

She frowns at the strange word. 'We did Adrienne Rich and Toni Morrison in my second year. And Alice Walker. I got pretty involved. But I wouldn't call it a passion exactly.'

So: not a creature of passion. In the most roundabout of ways, is she warning him off?

'I am going to throw together some supper,' he says. 'Will you join me? It will be very simple.'

She looks dubious.

'Come on!' he says. 'Say yes!'

'OK. But I have to make a phone call first.'

The call takes longer than he expected. From the kitchen he hears murmurings, silences.

'What are your career plans?' he asks afterwards.

'Stagecraft and design. I'm doing a diploma in theatre.'

'And what is your reason for taking a course in Romantic poetry?'

She ponders, wrinkling her nose. 'It's mainly for the atmosphere that I chose it,' she says. 'I didn't want to take Shakespeare again. I took Shakespeare last year.'

What he throws together for supper is indeed simple: anchovies on tagliatelle with a mushroom sauce. He lets her chop the mushrooms. Otherwise she sits on a stool, watching while he cooks. They eat in the dining-room, opening a second bottle of wine. She eats without inhibition. A healthy appetite, for someone so slight.

'Do you always cook for yourself?' she asks.

'I live alone. If I don't cook, no one will.'

'I hate cooking. I guess I should learn.'

'Why? If you really hate it, marry a man who cooks.'

Together they contemplate the picture: the young wife with the daring clothes and gaudy jewellery striding through the front door, impatiently sniffing the air; the husband, colourless Mr Right, aproned, stirring a pot in the steaming kitchen. Reversals: the stuff of bourgeois comedy.

'That's all,' he says at the end, when the bowl is empty. 'No dessert, unless you want an apple or some yoghurt. Sorry – I didn't know I would be having a guest.'

'It was nice,' she says, draining her glass, rising. 'Thanks.'

'Don't go yet.' He takes her by the hand and leads her to the sofa. 'I have something to show you. Do you like dance? Not dancing: dance.' He slips a cassette into the video machine. 'It's a film by a man named Norman McLaren. It's quite old. I found it in the library. See what you think.'

Sitting side by side they watch. Two dancers on a bare stage

14

move through their steps. Recorded by a stroboscopic camera, their images, ghosts of their movements, fan out behind them like wingbeats. It is a film he first saw a quarter of a century ago but is still captivated by: the instant of the present and the past of that instant, evanescent, caught in the same space.

He wills the girl to be captivated too. But he senses she is not.

When the film is over she gets up and wanders around the room. She raises the lid of the piano, strikes middle C. 'Do you play?' she says.

'A bit.'

'Classics or jazz?'

'No jazz, I'm afraid.'

'Will you play something for me?'

'Not now. I'm out of practice. Another time, when we know each other better.'

She peers into his study. 'Can I look?' she says.

'Switch on the light.'

He puts on more music: Scarlatti sonatas, cat-music.

'You've got a lot of Byron books,' she says when she comes out. 'Is he your favourite?'

'I'm working on Byron. On his time in Italy.'

'Didn't he die young?'

'Thirty-six. They all died young. Or dried up. Or went mad and were locked away. But Italy wasn't where Byron died. He died in Greece. He went to Italy to escape a scandal, and settled there. Settled down. Had the last big love-affair of his life. Italy was a popular destination for the English in those days. They believed the Italians were still in touch with their natures. Less hemmed in by convention, more passionate.'

She makes another circuit of the room. 'Is this your wife?' she asks, stopping before the framed photograph on the coffee-table.

'My mother. Taken when she was young.'

15

'Are you married?'

'I was. Twice. But now I'm not.' He does not say: Now I make do with what comes my way. He does not say: Now I make do with whores. 'Can I offer you a liqueur?'

She does not want a liqueur, but does accept a shot of whisky in her coffee. As she sips, he leans over and touches her cheek. 'You're very lovely,' he says. 'I'm going to invite you to do something reckless.' He touches her again. 'Stay. Spend the night with me.'

Across the rim of the cup she regards him steadily. 'Why?'

'Because you ought to.'

'Why ought I to?'

'Why? Because a woman's beauty does not belong to her alone. It is part of the bounty she brings into the world. She has a duty to share it.'

His hand still rests against her cheek. She does not withdraw, but does not yield either.

'And what if I already share it?' In her voice there is a hint of breathlessness. Exciting, always, to be courted: exciting, pleasurable.

'Then you should share it more widely.'

Smooth words, as old as seduction itself. Yet at this moment he believes in them. She does not own herself. Beauty does not own itself.

'From fairest creatures we desire increase,' he says, 'that thereby beauty's rose might never die.'

Not a good move. Her smile loses its playful, mobile quality. The pentameter, whose cadence once served so well to oil the serpent's words, now only estranges. He has become a teacher again, man of the book, guardian of the culture-hoard. She puts down her cup. 'I must leave, I'm expected.'

The clouds have cleared, the stars are shining. 'A lovely night,' he says, unlocking the garden gate. She does not look up. 'Shall I walk you home?'

'No.'

'Very well. Good night.' He reaches out, enfolds her. For a moment he can feel her little breasts against him. Then she slips his embrace and is gone.

THREE

THAT IS WHERE he ought to end it. But he does not. On Sunday morning he drives to the empty campus and lets himself into the department office. From the filing cabinet he extracts Melanie Isaacs's enrolment card and copies down her personal details: home address, Cape Town address, telephone number.

He dials the number. A woman's voice answers.

'Melanie?'

'I'll call her. Who is speaking?'

'Tell her, David Lurie.'

Melanie – melody: a meretricious rhyme. Not a good name for her. Shift the accent. Meláni: the dark one.

'Hello?'

In the one word he hears all her uncertainty. Too young. She will not know how to deal with him; he ought to let her go. But he is in the grip of something. Beauty's rose: the poem drives straight as an arrow. She does not own herself; perhaps he does not own himself either.

'I thought you might like to go out to lunch,' he says. 'I'll pick you up at, shall we say, twelve.'

There is still time for her to tell a lie, wriggle out. But she is too confused, and the moment passes.

When he arrives, she is waiting on the sidewalk outside her

apartment block. She is wearing black tights and a black sweater. Her hips are as slim as a twelve-year-old's.

He takes her to Hout Bay, to the harbourside. During the drive he tries to put her at ease. He asks about her other courses. She is acting in a play, she says. It is one of her diploma requirements. Rehearsals are taking up a lot of her time.

At the restaurant she has no appetite, stares out glumly over the sea.

'Is something the matter? Do you want to tell me?'

She shakes her head.

'Are you worried about the two of us?'

'Maybe,' she says.

'No need. I'll take care. I won't let it go too far.'

Too far. What is far, what is too far, in a matter like this? Is her too far the same as his too far?

It has begun to rain: sheets of water waver across the empty bay. 'Shall we leave?' he says.

He takes her back to his house. On the living-room floor, to the sound of rain pattering against the windows, he makes love to her. Her body is clear, simple, in its way perfect; though she is passive throughout, he finds the act pleasurable, so pleasurable that from its climax he tumbles into blank oblivion.

When he comes back the rain has stopped. The girl is lying beneath him, her eyes closed, her hands slack above her head, a slight frown on her face. His own hands are under her coarse-knit sweater, on her breasts. Her tights and panties lie in a tangle on the floor; his trousers are around his ankles. *After the storm*, he thinks: straight out of George Grosz.

Averting her face, she frees herself, gathers her things, leaves the room. In a few minutes she is back, dressed. 'I must go,' she whispers. He makes no effort to detain her.

He wakes the next morning in a state of profound wellbeing,

which does not go away. Melanie is not in class. From his office he telephones a florist. Roses? Perhaps not roses. He orders carnations. 'Red or white?' asks the woman. Red? White? 'Send twelve pink,' he says. 'I haven't got twelve pink. Shall I send a mix?' 'Send a mix,' he says.

Rain falls all of Tuesday, from heavy clouds blown in over the city from the west. Crossing the lobby of the Communications Building at the end of the day, he spies her at the doorway amid a knot of students waiting for a break in the downpour. He comes up behind her, puts a hand on her shoulder. 'Wait for me here,' he says. 'I'll give you a ride home.'

He returns with an umbrella. Crossing the square to the parking lot he draws her closer to shelter her. A sudden gust blows the umbrella inside out; awkwardly they run together to the car.

She is wearing a slick yellow raincoat; in the car she lowers the hood. Her face is flushed; he is aware of the rise and fall of her chest. She licks away a drop of rain from her upper lip. *A child!* he thinks: *No more than a child! What am I doing?* Yet his heart lurches with desire.

They drive through dense late-afternoon traffic. 'I missed you yesterday,' he says. 'Are you all right?'

She does not reply, staring at the wiper blades.

At a red light he takes her cold hand in his. 'Melanie!' he says, trying to keep his tone light. But he has forgotten how to woo. The voice he hears belongs to a cajoling parent, not a lover.

He draws up before her apartment block. 'Thanks,' she says, opening the car door.

'Aren't you going to invite me in?'

'I think my flatmate is home.'

'What about this evening?'

'I've got a rehearsal this evening.'

'Then when do I see you again?'

She does not answer. 'Thanks,' she repeats, and slides out.

On Wednesday she is in class, in her usual seat. They are still on Wordsworth, on Book 6 of *The Prelude*, the poet in the Alps.

'From a bare ridge,' he reads aloud,

> we also first beheld
> Unveiled the summit of Mont Blanc, and grieved
> To have a soulless image on the eye
> That had usurped upon a living thought
> That never more could be.

'So. The majestic white mountain, Mont Blanc, turns out to be a disappointment. Why? Let us start with the unusual verb form *usurp upon*. Did anyone look it up in a dictionary?'

Silence.

'If you had, you would have found that *usurp upon* means to intrude or encroach upon. *Usurp*, to take over entirely, is the perfective of *usurp upon*; usurping completes the act of usurping upon.

'The clouds cleared, says Wordsworth, the peak was unveiled, and we grieved to see it. A strange response, for a traveller to the Alps. Why grieve? Because, he says, a soulless image, a mere image on the retina, has encroached upon what has hitherto been a living thought. What was that living thought?'

Silence again. The very air into which he speaks hangs listless as a sheet. A man looking at a mountain: why does it have to be so complicated, they want to complain? What answer can he give them? What did he say to Melanie that first evening? That without a flash of revelation there is nothing. Where is the flash of revelation in this room?

21

He casts a quick glance at her. Her head is bowed, she is absorbed in the text, or seems to be.

'The same word *usurp* recurs a few lines later. Usurpation is one of the deeper themes of the Alps sequence. The great archetypes of the mind, pure ideas, find themselves usurped by mere sense-images.

'Yet we cannot live our daily lives in a realm of pure ideas, cocooned from sense-experience. The question is not, How can we keep the imagination pure, protected from the onslaughts of reality? The question has to be, Can we find a way for the two to coexist?

'Look at line 599. Wordsworth is writing about the limits of sense-perception. It is a theme we have touched on before. As the sense-organs reach the limit of their powers, their light begins to go out. Yet at the moment of expiry that light leaps up one last time like a candle-flame, giving us a glimpse of the invisible. The passage is difficult; perhaps it even contradicts the Mont Blanc moment. Nevertheless, Wordsworth seems to be feeling his way toward a balance: not the pure idea, wreathed in clouds, nor the visual image burned on the retina, overwhelming and disappointing us with its matter-of-fact clarity, but the sense-image, kept as fleeting as possible, as a means toward stirring or activating the idea that lies buried more deeply in the soil of memory.'

He pauses. Blank incomprehension. He has gone too far too fast. How to bring them to him? How to bring her?

'Like being in love,' he says. 'If you were blind you would hardly have fallen in love in the first place. But now, do you truly wish to see the beloved in the cold clarity of the visual apparatus? It may be in your better interest to throw a veil over the gaze, so as to keep her alive in her archetypal, goddesslike form.'

It is hardly in Wordsworth, but at least it wakes them up.

Archetypes? they are saying to themselves. *Goddesses? What is he talking about? What does this old man know about love?*

A memory floods back: the moment on the floor when he forced the sweater up and exposed her neat, perfect little breasts. For the first time she looks up; her eyes meet his and in a flash see all. Confused, she drops her glance.

'Wordsworth is writing about the Alps,' he says. 'We don't have Alps in this country, but we have the Drakensberg, or on a smaller scale Table Mountain, which we climb in the wake of the poets, hoping for one of those revelatory, Wordsworthian moments we have all heard about.' Now he is just talking, covering up. 'But moments like that will not come unless the eye is half turned toward the great archetypes of the imagination we carry within us.'

Enough! He is sick of the sound of his own voice, and sorry for her too, having to listen to these covert intimacies. He dismisses the class, then lingers, hoping for a word with her. But she slips away in the throng.

A week ago she was just another pretty face in the class. Now she is a presence in his life, a breathing presence.

The auditorium of the student union is in darkness. Unnoticed, he takes a seat in the back row. Save for a balding man in a janitor's uniform a few rows in front of him, he is the only spectator.

Sunset at the Globe Salon is the name of the play they are rehearsing: a comedy of the new South Africa set in a hairdressing salon in Hillbrow, Johannesburg. On stage a hairdresser, flamboyantly gay, attends to two clients, one black, one white. Patter passes among the three of them: jokes, insults. Catharsis seems to be the presiding principle: all the coarse old prejudices brought into the light of day and washed away in gales of laughter.

A fourth figure comes onstage, a girl in high platform shoes with her hair done in a cascade of ringlets. 'Take a seat, dearie, I'll attend

23

to you in a mo,' says the hairdresser. 'I've come for the job,' she replies – 'the one you advertised.' Her accent is glaringly *Kaaps*; it is Melanie. '*Ag*, pick up a broom and make yourself useful,' says the hairdresser.

She picks up a broom, totters around the set pushing it before her. The broom gets tangled in an electric cord. There is supposed to be a flash, followed by a screaming and a scurrying around, but something goes wrong with the synchronization. The director comes striding onstage, and behind her a young man in black leather who begins to fiddle with the wall-socket. 'It's got to be snappier,' says the director. 'A more Marx Brothers atmosphere.' She turns to Melanie. 'OK?' Melanie nods.

Ahead of him the janitor stands up and with a heavy sigh leaves the auditorium. He ought to be gone too. An unseemly business, sitting in the dark spying on a girl (unbidden the word *letching* comes to him). Yet the old men whose company he seems to be on the point of joining, the tramps and drifters with their stained raincoats and cracked false teeth and hairy earholes – all of them were once upon a time children of God, with straight limbs and clear eyes. Can they be blamed for clinging to the last to their place at the sweet banquet of the senses?

Onstage the action resumes. Melanie pushes her broom. A bang, a flash, screams of alarm. 'It's not my fault,' squawks Melanie. '*My gats*, why must everything always be my fault?' Quietly he gets up, follows the janitor into the darkness outside.

At four o'clock the next afternoon he is at her flat. She opens the door wearing a crumpled T-shirt, cycling shorts, slippers in the shape of comic-book gophers which he finds silly, tasteless.

He has given her no warning; she is too surprised to resist the intruder who thrusts himself upon her. When he takes her in his arms, her limbs crumple like a marionette's. Words heavy as clubs thud into the delicate whorl of her ear. 'No, not now!' she says, struggling. 'My cousin will be back!'

But nothing will stop him. He carries her to the bedroom, brushes off the absurd slippers, kisses her feet, astonished by the feeling she evokes. Something to do with the apparition on the stage: the wig, the wiggling bottom, the crude talk. Strange love! Yet from the quiver of Aphrodite, goddess of the foaming waves, no doubt about that.

She does not resist. All she does is avert herself: avert her lips, avert her eyes. She lets him lay her out on the bed and undress her: she even helps him, raising her arms and then her hips. Little shivers of cold run through her; as soon as she is bare, she slips under the quilted counterpane like a mole burrowing, and turns her back on him.

Not rape, not quite that, but undesired nevertheless, undesired to the core. As though she had decided to go slack, die within herself for the duration, like a rabbit when the jaws of the fox close on its neck. So that everything done to her might be done, as it were, far away.

'Pauline will be back any minute,' she says when it is over. 'Please. You must go.'

He obeys, but then, when he reaches his car, is overtaken with such dejection, such dullness, that he sits slumped at the wheel unable to move.

A mistake, a huge mistake. At this moment, he has no doubt, she, Melanie, is trying to cleanse herself of it, of him. He sees her running a bath, stepping into the water, eyes closed like a sleepwalker's. He would like to slide into a bath of his own.

A woman with chunky legs and a no-nonsense business suit passes by and enters the apartment block. Is this cousin Pauline the flatmate, the one whose disapproval Melanie is so afraid of? He rouses himself, drives off.

The next day she is not in class. An unfortunate absence, since it is the day of the mid-term test. When he fills in the register afterwards, he ticks her off as present and enters a mark of seventy. At the foot of the page he pencils a note to himself: 'Provisional'. Seventy: a vacillator's mark, neither good nor bad.

She stays away the whole of the next week. Time after time he telephones, without reply. Then at midnight on Sunday the doorbell rings. It is Melanie, dressed from top to toe in black, with a little black woollen cap. Her face is strained; he steels himself for angry words, for a scene.

The scene does not come. In fact, she is the one who is embarrassed. 'Can I sleep here tonight?' she whispers, avoiding his eye.

'Of course, of course.' His heart is flooded with relief. He reaches out, embraces her, pressing her against him stiff and cold. 'Come, I'll make you some tea.'

'No, no tea, nothing, I'm exhausted, I just need to crash.'

He makes up a bed for her in his daughter's old room, kisses her good night, leaves her to herself. When he returns half an hour later she is in a dead sleep, fully clothed. He eases off her shoes, covers her.

At seven in the morning, as the first birds are beginning to chirrup, he knocks at her door. She is awake, lying with the sheet drawn up to her chin, looking haggard.

'How are you feeling?' he asks.

She shrugs.

'Is something the matter? Do you want to talk?'

She shakes her head mutely.

He sits down on the bed, draws her to him. In his arms she begins to sob miserably. Despite all, he feels a tingling of desire. 'There, there,' he whispers, trying to comfort her. 'Tell me what is wrong.' Almost he says, 'Tell Daddy what is wrong.'

She gathers herself and tries to speak, but her nose is clogged. He finds her a tissue. 'Can I stay here a while?' she says.

'Stay here?' he repeats carefully. She has stopped crying, but long shudders of misery still pass through her. 'Would that be a good idea?'

Whether it would be a good idea she does not say. Instead she presses herself tighter to him, her face warm against his belly. The sheet slips aside; she is wearing only a singlet and panties.

Does she know what she is up to, at this moment?

When he made the first move, in the college gardens, he had thought of it as a quick little affair – quickly in, quickly out. Now here she is in his house, trailing complications behind her. What game is she playing? He should be wary, no doubt about that. But he should have been wary from the start.

He stretches out on the bed beside her. The last thing in the world he needs is for Melanie Isaacs to take up residence with him. Yet at this moment the thought is intoxicating. Every night she will be here; every night he can slip into her bed like this, slip into her. People will find out, they always do; there will be whispering, there might even be scandal. But what will that matter? A last leap of the flame of sense before it goes out. He folds the bedclothes aside, reaches down, strokes her breasts, her buttocks. 'Of course you can stay,' he murmurs. 'Of course.'

In his bedroom, two doors away, the alarm clock goes off. She turns away from him, pulls the covers up over her shoulders.

'I'm going to leave now,' he says. 'I have classes to meet. Try to sleep again. I'll be back at noon, then we can talk.' He strokes her hair, kisses her forehead. Mistress? Daughter? What, in her heart, is she trying to be? What is she offering him?

When he returns at noon, she is up, sitting at the kitchen table, eating toast and honey and drinking tea. She seems thoroughly at home.

'So,' he says, 'you are looking much better.'

'I slept after you left.'

'Will you tell me now what this is all about?'

She avoids his eye. 'Not now,' she says. 'I have to go, I'm late. I'll explain next time.'

'And when will next time be?'

'This evening, after rehearsal. Is that OK?'

'Yes.'

She gets up, carries her cup and plate to the sink (but does not wash them), turns to face him. 'Are you sure it's OK?' she says.

'Yes, it's OK.'

'I wanted to say, I know I've missed a lot of classes, but the production is taking up all my time.'

'I understand. You are telling me your drama work has priority. It would have helped if you had explained earlier. Will you be in class tomorrow?'

'Yes. I promise.'

She promises, but with a promise that is not enforceable. He is vexed, irritated. She is behaving badly, getting away with too much; she is learning to exploit him and will probably exploit him further. But if she has got away with much, he has got away with more; if she is behaving badly, he has behaved worse. To the extent that they are together, if they are together, he is the one who leads, she the one who follows. Let him not forget that.

FOUR

HE MAKES LOVE to her one more time, on the bed in his daughter's room. It is good, as good as the first time; he is beginning to learn the way her body moves. She is quick, and greedy for experience. If he does not sense in her a fully sexual appetite, that is only because she is still young. One moment stands out in recollection, when she hooks a leg behind his buttocks to draw him in closer: as the tendon of her inner thigh tightens against him, he feels a surge of joy and desire. Who knows, he thinks: there might, despite all, be a future.

'Do you do this kind of thing often?' she asks afterwards.

'Do what?'

'Sleep with your students. Have you slept with Amanda?'

He does not answer. Amanda is another student in the class, a wispy blonde. He has no interest in Amanda.

'Why did you get divorced?' she asks.

'I've been divorced twice. Married twice, divorced twice.'

'What happened to your first wife?'

'It's a long story. I'll tell you some other time.'

'Do you have pictures?'

'I don't collect pictures. I don't collect women.'

'Aren't you collecting me?'

'No, of course not.'

She gets up, strolls around the room picking up her clothes, as little bashful as if she were alone. He is used to women more self-conscious in their dressing and undressing. But the women he is used to are not as young, as perfectly formed.

The same afternoon there is a knock at his office door and a young man enters whom he has not seen before. Without invitation he sits down, casts a look around the room, nods appreciatively at the bookcases.

He is tall and wiry; he has a thin goatee and an ear-ring; he wears a black leather jacket and black leather trousers. He looks older than most students; he looks like trouble.

'So you are the professor,' he says. 'Professor David. Melanie has told me about you.'

'Indeed. And what has she told you?'

'That you fuck her.'

There is a long silence. So, he thinks: the chickens come home to roost. I should have guessed it: a girl like that would not come unencumbered.

'Who are you?' he says.

The visitor ignores his question. 'You think you're smart,' he continues. 'A real ladies' man. You think you will still look so smart when your wife hears what you are up to?'

'That's enough. What do you want?'

'Don't you tell me what's enough.' The words come faster now, in a patter of menace. 'And don't think you can just walk into people's lives and walk out again when it suits you.' Light dances on his black eyeballs. He leans forward, sweeps right and left with his hands. The papers on the desk go flying.

He rises. 'That's enough! It's time for you to leave!'

'*It's time for you to leave!*' the boy repeats, mimicking him.

'OK.' He gets up, saunters to the door. 'Goodbye, Professor Chips! But just wait and see!' Then he is gone.

A bravo, he thinks. She is mixed up with a bravo and now I am mixed up with her bravo too! His stomach churns.

Though he stays up late into the night, waiting for her, Melanie does not come. Instead, his car, parked in the street, is vandalized. The tyres are deflated, glue is injected into the doorlocks, newspaper is pasted over the windscreen, the paintwork is scratched. The locks have to be replaced; the bill comes to six hundred rand.

'Any idea who did it?' asks the locksmith.

'None at all,' he replies curtly.

After this *coup de main* Melanie keeps her distance. He is not surprised: if he has been shamed, she is shamed too. But on Monday she reappears in class; and beside her, leaning back in his seat, hands in pockets, with an air of cocky ease, is the boy in black, the boyfriend.

Usually there is a buzz of talk from the students. Today there is a hush. Though he cannot believe they know what is afoot, they are clearly waiting to see what he will do about the intruder.

What will he do indeed? What happened to his car was evidently not enough. Evidently there are more instalments to come. What can he do? He must grit his teeth and pay, what else?

'We continue with Byron,' he says, plunging into his notes. 'As we saw last week, notoriety and scandal affected not only Byron's life but the way in which his poems were received by the public. Byron the man found himself conflated with his own poetic creations – with Harold, Manfred, even Don Juan.'

Scandal. A pity that must be his theme, but he is in no state to improvise.

He steals a glance at Melanie. Usually she is a busy writer.

Today, looking thin and exhausted, she sits huddled over her book. Despite himself, his heart goes out to her. Poor little bird, he thinks, whom I have held against my breast!

He has told them to read 'Lara'. His notes deal with 'Lara'. There is no way in which he can evade the poem. He reads aloud:

> He stood a stranger in this breathing world,
> An erring spirit from another hurled;
> A thing of dark imaginings, that shaped
> By choice the perils he by chance escaped.

'Who will gloss these lines for me? Who is this "erring spirit"? Why does he call himself "a thing"? From what world does he come?'

He has long ceased to be surprised at the range of ignorance of his students. Post-Christian, posthistorical, postliterate, they might as well have been hatched from eggs yesterday. So he does not expect them to know about fallen angels or where Byron might have read of them. What he does expect is a round of goodnatured guesses which, with luck, he can guide toward the mark. But today he is met with silence, a dogged silence that organizes itself palpably around the stranger in their midst. They will not speak, they will not play his game, as long as a stranger is there to listen and judge and mock.

'Lucifer,' he says. 'The angel hurled out of heaven. Of how angels live we know little, but we can assume they do not require oxygen. At home Lucifer, the dark angel, does not need to breathe. All of a sudden he finds himself cast out into this strange "breathing world" of ours. "Erring": a being who chooses his own path, who lives dangerously, even creating danger for himself. Let us read further.'

The boy has not looked down once at the text. Instead, with a little smile on his lips, a smile in which there is, just possibly, a touch of bemusement, he takes in his words.

> He could
> At times resign his own for others' good,
> But not in pity, not because he ought,
> But in some strange perversity of thought,
> That swayed him onward with a secret pride
> To do what few or none would do beside;
> And this same impulse would in tempting time
> Mislead his spirit equally to crime.

'So, what kind of creature is this Lucifer?'

By now the students must surely feel the current running between them, between himself and the boy. It is to the boy alone that the question has addressed itself; and, like a sleeper summoned to life, the boy responds. 'He does what he feels like. He doesn't care if it's good or bad. He just does it.'

'Exactly. Good or bad, he just does it. He doesn't act on principle but on impulse, and the source of his impulses is dark to him. Read a few lines further: "His madness was not of the head, but heart." A mad heart. What is a mad heart?'

He is asking too much. The boy would like to press his intuition further, he can see that. He wants to show that he knows about more than just motorcycles and flashy clothes. And perhaps he does. Perhaps he does indeed have intimations of what it is to have a mad heart. But, here, in this classroom, before these strangers, the words will not come. He shakes his head.

'Never mind. Note that we are not asked to condemn this being with the mad heart, this being with whom there is something constitutionally wrong. On the contrary, we are invited to understand and sympathize. But there is a limit to sympathy. For though

33

he lives among us, he is not one of us. He is exactly what he calls himself: a *thing*, that is, a monster. Finally, Byron will suggest, it will not be possible to love him, not in the deeper, more human sense of the word. He will be condemned to solitude.'

Heads bent, they scribble down his words. Byron, Lucifer, Cain, it is all the same to them.

They finish the poem. He assigns the first cantos of *Don Juan* and ends the class early. Across their heads he calls to her: 'Melanie, can I have a word with you?'

Pinch-faced, exhausted, she stands before him. Again his heart goes out to her. If they were alone he would embrace her, try to cheer her up. *My little dove*, he would call her.

'Shall we go to my office?' he says instead.

With the boyfriend trailing behind, he leads her up the stairway to his office. 'Wait here,' he tells the boy, and closes the door on him.

Melanie sits before him, her head sunken. 'My dear,' he says, 'you are going through a difficult time, I know that, and I don't want to make it more difficult. But I must speak to you as a teacher. I have obligations to my students, all of them. What your friend does off campus is his own business. But I can't have him disrupting my classes. Tell him that, from me.

'As for yourself, you are going to have to give more time to your work. You are going to have to attend class more regularly. And you are going to have to make up the test you missed.'

She stares back at him in puzzlement, even shock. *You have cut me off from everyone*, she seems to want to say. *You have made me bear your secret. I am no longer just a student. How can you speak to me like this?*

Her voice, when it comes, is so subdued that he can barely hear: 'I can't take the test, I haven't done the reading.'

What he wants to say cannot be said, not decently. All he can

34

do is signal, and hope that she understands. 'Just take the test, Melanie, like everyone else. It does not matter if you are not prepared, the point is to get it behind you. Let us set a date. How about next Monday, during the lunch break? That will give you the weekend to do the reading.'

She raises her chin, meets his eye defiantly. Either she has not understood or she is refusing the opening.

'Monday, here in my office,' he repeats.

She rises, slings her bag over her shoulder.

'Melanie, I have responsibilities. At least go through the motions. Don't make the situation more complicated than it need be.'

Responsibilities: she does not dignify the word with a reply.

Driving home from a concert that evening, he stops at a traffic light. A motorcycle throbs past, a silver Ducati bearing two figures in black. They wear helmets, but he recognizes them nevertheless. Melanie, on the pillion, sits with knees wide apart, pelvis arched. A quick shudder of lust tugs him. *I have been there!* he thinks. Then the motorcycle surges forward, bearing her away.

FIVE

SHE DOES NOT appear for her examination on Monday. Instead, in his mailbox he finds an official withdrawal card: Student 7710101SAM Ms M Isaacs has withdrawn from COM 312 with immediate effect.

Barely an hour later a telephone call is switched through to his office. 'Professor Lurie? Have you a moment to talk? My name is Isaacs, I'm calling from George. My daughter is in your class, you know, Melanie.'

'Yes.'

'Professor, I wonder if you can help us. Melanie has been such a good student, and now she says she is going to give it all up. It has come as a terrible shock to us.'

'I'm not sure I understand.'

'She wants to give up her studies and get a job. It seems such a waste, to spend three years at university and do so well, and then drop out before the end. I wonder if I can ask, Professor, can you have a chat with her, talk some sense into her?'

'Have you spoken to Melanie yourself? Do you know what is behind this decision?'

'We spent all weekend on the phone to her, her mother and I, but we just can't get sense out of her. She is very involved in a play she is acting in, so maybe she is, you know, overworked,

36

overstressed. She always takes things so to heart, Professor, that's her nature, she gets very involved. But if you talk to her, maybe you can persuade her to think again. She has such respect for you. We don't want her to throw away all these years for nothing.'

So Melanie-Meláni, with her baubles from the Oriental Plaza and her blind spot for Wordsworth, takes things to heart. He would not have guessed it. What else has he not guessed about her?

'I wonder, Mr Isaacs, whether I am the right person to speak to Melanie.'

'You are, Professor, you are! As I say, Melanie has such respect for you.'

Respect? You are out of date, Mr Isaacs. Your daughter lost respect for me weeks ago, and with good reason. That is what he ought to say. 'I'll see what I can do,' he says instead.

You will not get away with it, he tells himself afterwards. Nor will father Isaacs in faraway George forget this conversation, with its lies and evasions. *I'll see what I can do.* Why not come clean? *I am the worm in the apple,* he should have said. *How can I help you when I am the very source of your woe?*

He telephones the flat and gets cousin Pauline. Melanie is not available, says Pauline in a chilly voice. 'What do you mean, not available?' 'I mean she doesn't want to speak to you.' 'Tell her', he says, 'it is about her decision to withdraw. Tell her she is being very rash.'

Wednesday's class goes badly, Friday's even worse. Attendance is poor; the only students who come are the tame ones, the passive, the docile. There can be only one explanation. The story must be out.

He is in the department office when he hears a voice behind him: 'Where can I find Professor Lurie?'

'Here I am,' he says without thinking.

The man who has spoken is small, thin, stoop-shouldered.

37

He wears a blue suit too large for him, he smells of cigarette smoke.

'Professor Lurie? We spoke on the telephone. Isaacs.'

'Yes. How do you do. Shall we go to my office?'

'That won't be necessary.' The man pauses, gathers himself, takes a deep breath. 'Professor,' he begins, laying heavy stress on the word, 'you may be very educated and all that, but what you have done is not right.' He pauses, shakes his head. 'It is not right.'

The two secretaries do not pretend to hide their curiosity. There are students in the office too; as the stranger's voice rises they fall silent.

'We put our children in the hands of you people because we think we can trust you. If we can't trust the university, who can we trust? We never thought we were sending our daughter into a nest of vipers. No, Professor Lurie, you may be high and mighty and have all kinds of degrees, but if I was you I'd be very ashamed of myself, so help me God. If I've got hold of the wrong end of the stick, now is your chance to say, but I don't think so, I can see it from your face.'

Now is his chance indeed: let him who would speak, speak. But he stands tongue-tied, the blood thudding in his ears. A viper: how can he deny it?

'Excuse me,' he whispers, 'I have business to attend to.' Like a thing of wood, he turns and leaves.

Into the crowded corridor Isaacs follows him. 'Professor! Professor Lurie!' he calls. 'You can't just run away like that! You have not heard the last of it, I tell you now!'

That is how it begins. Next morning, with surprising dispatch, a memorandum arrives from the office of the Vice-Rector (Student Affairs) notifying him that a complaint has been lodged against him under article 3.1 of the university's Code of Conduct. He is requested to contact the Vice-Rector's office at his earliest convenience.

The notification – which arrives in an envelope marked *Confidential* – is accompanied by a copy of the code. Article 3 deals with victimization or harassment on grounds of race, ethnic group, religion, gender, sexual preference, or physical disability. Article 3.1 addresses victimization or harassment of students by teachers.

A second document describes the constitution and competences of committees of inquiry. He reads it, his heart hammering unpleasantly. Halfway through, his concentration fails. He gets up, locks the door of his office, and sits with the paper in his hand, trying to imagine what has happened.

Melanie would not have taken such a step by herself, he is convinced. She is too innocent for that, too ignorant of her power. He, the little man in the ill-fitting suit, must be behind it, he and cousin Pauline, the plain one, the duenna. They must have talked her into it, worn her down, then in the end marched her to the administration offices.

'We want to lodge a complaint,' they must have said.

'Lodge a complaint? What kind of complaint?'

'It's private.'

'Harassment,' cousin Pauline would have interjected, while Melanie stood by abashed – 'against a professor.'

'Go to room such-and-such.'

In room such-and-such he, Isaacs, would grow bolder. 'We want to lay a complaint against one of your professors.'

'Have you thought it through? Is this really what you want to do?' they would respond, following procedure.

'Yes, we know what we want to do,' he would say, glancing at his daughter, daring her to object.

There is a form to fill in. The form is placed before them, and a pen. A hand takes up the pen, a hand he has kissed, a hand he knows intimately. First the name of the plaintiff: MELANIE ISAACS, in careful block letters. Down the column of boxes wavers the hand, searching for the one to tick. *There*, points the nicotine-stained finger of her father. The hand slows, settles, makes its X, its cross of righteousness: *J'accuse*. Then a space for the name of the accused. DAVID LURIE, writes the hand: PROFESSOR. Finally, at the foot of the page, the date and her signature: the arabesque of the *M*, the *l* with its bold upper loop, the downward gash of the *I*, the flourish of the final *s*.

The deed is done. Two names on the page, his and hers, side by side. Two in a bed, lovers no longer but foes.

He calls the Vice-Rector's office and is given a five o'clock appointment, outside regular hours.

At five o'clock he is waiting in the corridor. Aram Hakim, sleek and youthful, emerges and ushers him in. There are already two persons in the room: Elaine Winter, chair of his department, and Farodia Rassool from Social Sciences, who chairs the university-wide committee on discrimination.

'It's late, David, we know why we are here,' says Hakim, 'so let's get to the point. How can we best tackle this business?'

'You can fill me in about the complaint.'

'Very well. We are talking about a complaint laid by Ms Melanie Isaacs. Also about' – he glances at Elaine Winter – 'some pre-existing irregularities that seem to involve Ms Isaacs. Elaine?'

Elaine Winter takes her cue. She has never liked him; she regards him as a hangover from the past, the sooner cleared away the better. 'There is a query about Ms Isaacs's attendance, David. According to her – I spoke to her on the phone – she has attended only two classes in the past month. If that is true, it should have been reported. She also says she missed the mid-term test. Yet' – she glances at the file in front of her – 'according to your records, her attendance is unblemished and she has a mark of seventy for the mid-term.' She regards him quizzically. 'So unless there are two Melanie Isaacs . . .'

'There is only one,' he says. 'I have no defence.'

Smoothly Hakim intervenes. 'Friends, this is not the time or place to go into substantial issues. What we should do' – he glances at the other two – 'is clarify procedure. I need barely say, David, the matter will be handled in the strictest confidence, I can assure you of that. Your name will be protected, Ms Isaacs's name will be protected too. A committee will be set up. Its function will be to determine whether there are grounds for disciplinary measures. You or your legal representative will have an opportunity to challenge its composition. Its hearings will be held in camera. In the meantime, until the committee has made its recommendation to the Rector and the Rector has acted, everything goes on as before. Ms Isaacs has officially withdrawn from the course she takes with you, and you will be expected to refrain from all contact with her. Is there anything I am omitting, Farodia, Elaine?'

Tight-lipped, Dr Rassool shakes her head.

'It's always complicated, this harassment business, David, complicated as well as unfortunate, but we believe our procedures are good and fair, so we'll just take it step by step, play it by the book. My one suggestion is, acquaint yourself with the procedures and perhaps get legal advice.'

He is about to reply, but Hakim raises a warning hand. 'Sleep on it, David,' he says.

He has had enough. 'Don't tell me what to do, I'm not a child.'

He leaves in a fury. But the building is locked and the doorkeeper has gone home. The back exit is locked too. Hakim has to let him out.

It is raining. 'Share my umbrella,' says Hakim; then, at his car,

'Speaking personally, David, I want to tell you you have all my sympathy. Really. These things can be hell.'

He has known Hakim for years, they used to play tennis together in his tennis-playing days, but he is in no mood now for male chumminess. He shrugs irritably, gets into his car.

The case is supposed to be confidential, but of course it is not, of course people talk. Why else, when he enters the common-room, does a hush fall on the chatter, why does a younger colleague, with whom he has hitherto had perfectly cordial relations, put down her teacup and depart, looking straight through him as she passes? Why do only two students turn up for the first Baudelaire class?

The gossip-mill, he thinks, turning day and night, grinding reputations. The community of the righteous, holding their sessions in corners, over the telephone, behind closed doors. Gleeful whispers. *Schadenfreude*. First the sentence, then the trial.

In the corridors of the Communications Building he makes a point of walking with head held high.

He speaks to the lawyer who handled his divorce. 'Let's get it clear first,' says the lawyer, 'how true are the allegations?'

'True enough. I was having an affair with the girl.'

'Serious?'

'Does seriousness make it better or worse? After a certain age, all affairs are serious. Like heart attacks.'

'Well, my advice would be, as a matter of strategy, get a woman to represent you.' He mentions two names. 'Aim for a private settlement. You give certain undertakings, perhaps take a spell of leave, in return for which the university persuades the girl, or her family, to drop the charges. Your best hope. Take a yellow card. Minimize the damage, wait for the scandal to blow over.'

'What kind of undertakings?'

'Sensitivity training. Community service. Counselling. Whatever you can negotiate.'

'Counselling? I need counselling?'

'Don't misunderstand me. I'm simply saying that one of the options offered to you might be counselling.'

'To fix me? To cure me? To cure me of inappropriate desires?'

The lawyer shrugs. 'Whatever.'

On campus it is Rape Awareness Week. Women Against Rape, WAR, announces a twenty-four-hour vigil in solidarity with 'recent victims'. A pamphlet is slipped under his door: 'WOMEN SPEAK OUT.' Scrawled in pencil at the bottom is a message: 'YOUR DAYS ARE OVER, CASANOVA.'

He has dinner with his ex-wife Rosalind. They have been apart for eight years; slowly, warily, they are growing to be friends again, of a sort. War veterans. It reassures him that Rosalind still lives nearby: perhaps she feels the same way about him. Someone to count on when the worst arrives: the fall in the bathroom, the blood in the stool.

They speak of Lucy, sole issue of his first marriage, living now on a farm in the Eastern Cape. 'I may see her soon,' he says – 'I'm thinking of taking a trip.'

'In term time?'

'Term is nearly over. Another two weeks to get through, that's all.'

'Has this anything to do with the problems you are having? I hear you are having problems.'

'Where did you hear that?'

'People talk, David. Everyone knows about this latest affair of yours, in the juiciest detail. It's in no one's interest to hush it up, no one's but your own. Am I allowed to tell you how stupid it looks?'

'No, you are not.'

'I will anyway. Stupid, and ugly too. I don't know what you do about sex and I don't want to know, but this is not the way to go about it. You're what – fifty-two? Do you think a young girl finds any pleasure in going to bed with a man of that age? Do you think she finds it good to watch you in the middle of your...? Do you ever think about that?'

He is silent.

'Don't expect sympathy from me, David, and don't expect sympathy from anyone else either. No sympathy, no mercy, not in this day and age. Everyone's hand will be against you, and why not? Really, how *could* you?'

The old tone has entered, the tone of the last years of their married life: passionate recrimination. Even Rosalind must be aware of that. Yet perhaps she has a point. Perhaps it is the right of the young to be protected from the sight of their elders in the throes of passion. That is what whores are for, after all: to put up with the ecstasies of the unlovely.

'Anyway,' Rosalind goes on, 'you say you'll see Lucy.'

'Yes, I thought I'd drive up after the inquiry and spend some time with her.'

'The inquiry?'

'There is a committee of inquiry sitting next week.'

'That's very quick. And after you have seen Lucy?'

'I don't know. I'm not sure I will be permitted to come back to the university. I'm not sure I will want to.'

Rosalind shakes her head. 'An inglorious end to your career, don't you think? I won't ask if what you got from this girl was worth the price. What are you going to do with your time? What about your pension?'

'I'll come to some arrangement with them. They can't cut me off without a penny.'

'Can't they? Don't be so sure. How old is she – your inamorata?'

44

'Twenty. Of age. Old enough to know her own mind.'

'The story is, she took sleeping-pills. Is that true?'

'I know nothing about sleeping-pills. It sounds like a fabrication to me. Who told you about sleeping-pills?'

She ignores the question. 'Was she in love with you? Did you jilt her?'

'No. Neither.'

'Then why this complaint?'

'Who knows? She didn't confide in me. There was a battle of some kind going on behind the scenes that I wasn't privy to. There was a jealous boyfriend. There were indignant parents. She must have crumpled in the end. I was taken completely by surprise.'

'You should have known, David. You are too old to be meddling with other people's children. You should have expected the worst. Anyway, it's all very demeaning. Really.'

'You haven't asked whether I love her. Aren't you supposed to ask that as well?'

'Very well. Are you in love with this young woman who is dragging your name through the mud?'

'She isn't responsible. Don't blame her.'

'Don't blame her! Whose side are you on? Of course I blame her! I blame you and I blame her. The whole thing is disgraceful from beginning to end. Disgraceful and vulgar too. And I'm not sorry for saying so.'

In the old days he would, at this point, have stormed out. But tonight he does not. They have grown thick skins, he and Rosalind, against each other.

The next day Rosalind telephones. 'David, have you seen today's *Argus*?'

'No.'

'Well, steel yourself. There's a piece about you.'

'What does it say?'

45

'Read it for yourself.'

The report is on page three: 'Professor on sex charge', it is headed. He skims the first lines. '. . . is slated to appear before a disciplinary board on a charge of sexual harassment. CTU is keeping tight-lipped about the latest in a series of scandals including fraudulent scholarship payouts and alleged sex rings operating out of student residences. Lurie (53), author of a book on English nature-poet William Wordsworth, was not available for comment.'

William Wordsworth (1770–1850), nature-poet. David Lurie (1945–?), commentator upon, and disgraced disciple of, William Wordsworth. Blest be the infant babe. No outcast he. Blest be the babe.

SIX

THE HEARING IS held in a committee room off Hakim's office. He is ushered in and seated at the foot of the table by Manas Mathabane himself, Professor of Religious Studies, who will chair the inquiry. To his left sit Hakim, his secretary, and a young woman, a student of some kind; to his right are the three members of Mathabane's committee.

He does not feel nervous. On the contrary, he feels quite sure of himself. His heart beats evenly, he has slept well. Vanity, he thinks, the dangerous vanity of the gambler; vanity and self-righteousness. He is going into this in the wrong spirit. But he does not care.

He nods to the committee members. Two of them he knows: Farodia Rassool and Desmond Swarts, Dean of Engineering. The third, according to the papers in front of him, teaches in the Business School.

'The body here gathered, Professor Lurie,' says Mathabane, opening proceedings, 'has no powers. All it can do is to make recommendations. Furthermore, you have the right to challenge its makeup. So let me ask: is there any member of the committee whose participation you feel might be prejudicial to you?'

'I have no challenge in a legal sense,' he replies. 'I have reservations of a philosophical kind, but I suppose they are out of bounds.'

A general shifting and shuffling. 'I think we had better restrict ourself to the legal sense,' says Mathabane. 'You have no challenge to the makeup of the committee. Have you any objection to the presence of a student observer from the Coalition Against Discrimination?'

'I have no fear of the committee. I have no fear of the observer.'

'Very well. To the matter at hand. The first complainant is Ms Melanie Isaacs, a student in the drama programme, who has made a statement of which you all have copies. Do I need to summarize that statement? Professor Lurie?'

'Do I understand, Mr Chairman, that Ms Isaacs will not be appearing in person?'

'Ms Isaacs appeared before the committee yesterday. Let me remind you again, this is not a trial but an inquiry. Our rules of procedure are not those of a law court. Is that a problem for you?'

'No.'

'A second and related charge', Mathabane continues, 'comes from the Registrar, through the Office of Student Records, and concerns the validity of Ms Isaacs's record. The charge is that Ms Isaacs did not attend all the classes or submit all the written work or sit all the examinations for which you have given her credit.'

'That is the sum of it? Those are the charges?'

'They are.'

He takes a deep breath. 'I am sure the members of this committee have better things to do with their time than rehash a story over which there will be no dispute. I plead guilty to both charges. Pass sentence, and let us get on with our lives.'

Hakim leans across to Mathabane. Murmured words pass between them.

'Professor Lurie,' says Hakim, 'I must repeat, this is a committee of inquiry. Its role is to hear both sides of the case and make a recommendation. It has no power to take decisions. Again I ask, would it not be better if you were represented by someone familiar with our procedures?'

'I don't need representation. I can represent myself perfectly well. Do I understand that, despite the plea I have entered, we must continue with the hearing?'

'We want to give you an opportunity to state your position.'

'I have stated my position. I am guilty.'

'Guilty of what?'

'Of all that I am charged with.'

'You are taking us in circles, Professor Lurie.'

'Of everything Ms Isaacs avers, and of keeping false records.'

Now Farodia Rassool intervenes. 'You say you accept Ms Isaacs's statement, Professor Lurie, but have you actually read it?'

'I do not wish to read Ms Isaacs's statement. I accept it. I know of no reason why Ms Isaacs should lie.'

'But would it not be prudent to actually read the statement before accepting it?'

'No. There are more important things in life than being prudent.'

Farodia Rassool sits back in her seat. 'This is all very quixotic, Professor Lurie, but can you afford it? It seems to me we may have a duty to protect you from yourself.' She gives Hakim a wintry smile.

'You say you have not sought legal advice. Have you consulted anyone – a priest, for instance, or a counsellor? Would you be prepared to undergo counselling?'

The question comes from the young woman from the Business School. He can feel himself bristling. 'No, I have not sought counselling nor do I intend to seek it. I am a grown man. I am not receptive to being counselled. I am beyond the reach of counselling.' He turns to Mathabane. 'I have made my plea. Is there any reason why this debate should go on?'

There is a whispered consultation between Mathabane and Hakim.

'It has been proposed', says Mathabane, 'that the committee recess to discuss Professor Lurie's plea.'

A round of nods.

'Professor Lurie, could I ask you to step outside for a few minutes, you and Ms van Wyk, while we deliberate?'

He and the student observer retire to Hakim's office. No word passes between them; clearly the girl feels awkward. 'YOUR DAYS ARE OVER, CASANOVA.' What does she think of Casanova now that she meets him face to face?

They are called back in. The atmosphere in the room is not good: sour, it seems to him.

'So,' says Mathabane, 'to resume: Professor Lurie, you say you accept the truth of the charges brought against you?'

'I accept whatever Ms Isaacs alleges.'

'Dr Rassool, you have something you wish to say?'

'Yes. I want to register an objection to these responses of Professor Lurie's, which I regard as fundamentally evasive. Professor Lurie says he accepts the charges. Yet when we try to pin him down on what it is that he actually accepts, all we get is subtle mockery. To me that suggests that he accepts the charges only in name. In a case with overtones like this one, the wider community is entitled –'

He cannot let that go. 'There are no overtones in this case,' he snaps back.

'The wider community is entitled to know', she continues, raising her voice with practised ease, riding over him, 'what it is specifically that Professor Lurie acknowledges and therefore what it is that he is being censured for.'

Mathabane: 'If he is censured.'

'If he is censured. We fail to perform our duty if we are not crystal clear in our minds, and if we do not make it crystal clear in our recommendations, what Professor Lurie is being censured for.'

'In our own minds I believe we are crystal clear, Dr Rassool. The question is whether Professor Lurie is crystal clear in his mind.'

'Exactly. You have expressed exactly what I wanted to say.'

It would be wiser to shut up, but he does not. 'What goes on in my mind is my business, not yours, Farodia,' he says. 'Frankly, what you want from me is not a response but a confession. Well, I make no confession. I put forward a plea, as is my right. Guilty as charged. That is my plea. That is as far as I am prepared to go.'

'Mr Chair, I must protest. The issue goes beyond mere technicalities. Professor Lurie pleads guilty, but I ask myself, does he accept his guilt or is he simply going through the motions in the hope that the case will be buried under paper and forgotten? If he is simply going through the motions, I urge that we impose the severest penalty.'

'Let me remind you again, Dr Rassool,' says Mathabane, 'it is not up to us to impose penalties.'

'Then we should recommend the severest penalty. That Professor Lurie be dismissed with immediate effect and forfeit all benefits and privileges.'

'David?' The voice comes from Desmond Swarts, who has not spoken hitherto. 'David, are you sure you are handling the situation in the best way?' Swarts turns to the chair. 'Mr Chair, as I said while Professor Lurie was out of the room, I do believe that as members of a university community we ought not to proceed against a colleague in a coldly formalistic way. David, are you sure you don't want a postponement to give yourself time to reflect and perhaps consult?'

'Why? What do I need to reflect on?'

'On the gravity of your situation, which I am not sure you appreciate. To be blunt, you stand to lose your job. That's no joke in these days.'

'Then what do you advise me to do? Remove what Dr Rassool

calls the subtle mockery from my tone? Shed tears of contrition? What will be enough to save me?'

'You may find this hard to believe, David, but we around this table are not your enemies. We have our weak moments, all of us, we are only human. Your case is not unique. We would like to find a way for you to continue with your career.'

Easily Hakim joins in. 'We would like to help you, David, to find a way out of what must be a nightmare.'

They are his friends. They want to save him from his weakness, to wake him from his nightmare. They do not want to see him begging in the streets. They want him back in the classroom.

'In this chorus of goodwill,' he says, 'I hear no female voice.'

There is silence.

'Very well,' he says, 'let me confess. The story begins one evening, I forget the date, but not long past. I was walking through the old college gardens and so, it happened, was the young woman in question, Ms Isaacs. Our paths crossed. Words passed between us, and at that moment something happened which, not being a poet, I will not try to describe. Suffice it to say that Eros entered. After that I was not the same.'

'You were not the same as what?' asks the businesswoman cautiously.

'I was not myself. I was no longer a fifty-year-old divorcé at a loose end. I became a servant of Eros.'

'Is this a defence you are offering us? Ungovernable impulse?'

'It is not a defence. You want a confession, I give you a confession. As for the impulse, it was far from ungovernable. I have denied similar impulses many times in the past, I am ashamed to say.'

'Don't you think', says Swarts, 'that by its nature academic life must call for certain sacrifices? That for the good of the whole we have to deny ourselves certain gratifications?'

'You have in mind a ban on intimacy across the generations?'

52

'No, not necessarily. But as teachers we occupy positions of power. Perhaps a ban on mixing power relations with sexual relations. Which, I sense, is what was going on in this case. Or extreme caution.'

Farodia Rassool intervenes. 'We are again going round in circles, Mr Chair. Yes, he says, he is guilty; but when we try to get specificity, all of a sudden it is not abuse of a young woman he is confessing to, just an impulse he could not resist, with no mention of the pain he has caused, no mention of the long history of exploitation of which this is part. That is why I say it is futile to go on debating with Professor Lurie. We must take his plea at face value and recommend accordingly.'

Abuse: he was waiting for the word. Spoken in a voice quivering with righteousness. What does she see, when she looks at him, that keeps her at such a pitch of anger? A shark among the helpless little fishies? Or does she have another vision: of a great thick-boned male bearing down on a girl-child, a huge hand stifling her cries? How absurd! Then he remembers: they were gathered here yesterday in this same room, and she was before them, Melanie, who barely comes to his shoulder. Unequal: how can he deny that?

'I tend to agree with Dr Rassool,' says the businesswoman. 'Unless there is something that Professor Lurie wants to add, I think we should proceed to a decision.'

'Before we do that, Mr Chair,' says Swarts, 'I would like to plead with Professor Lurie one last time. Is there any form of statement he would be prepared to subscribe to?'

'Why? Why is it so important that I subscribe to a statement?'

'Because it would help to cool down what has become a very heated situation. Ideally we would all have preferred to resolve this case out of the glare of the media. But that has not been possible. It has received a lot of attention, it has acquired overtones that are beyond our control. All eyes are on the university to see how we handle it. I get the impression, listening to you, David, that you believe you are being treated unfairly. That is quite mistaken. We on this committee see ourselves as trying to work out a compromise which will allow you to keep your job. That is why I ask whether there is not a form of public statement that you could live with and that would allow us to recommend something less than the most severe sanction, namely, dismissal with censure.'

'You mean, will I humble myself and ask for clemency?'

Swarts sighs. 'David, it doesn't help to sneer at our efforts. At least accept an adjournment, so that you can think your position over.'

'What do you want the statement to contain?'

'An admission that you were wrong.'

'I have admitted that. Freely. I am guilty of the charges brought against me.'

'Don't play games with us, David. There is a difference between pleading guilty to a charge and admitting you were wrong, and you know that.'

'And that will satisfy you: an admission I was wrong?'

'No,' says Farodia Rassool. 'That would be back to front. *First* Professor Lurie must make his statement. *Then* we can decide whether to accept it in mitigation. We don't negotiate first on what should be in his statement. The statement should come from him, in his own words. Then we can see if it comes from his heart.'

'And you trust yourself to divine that, from the words I use – to divine whether it comes from my heart?'

'We will see what attitude you express. We will see whether you express contrition.'

'Very well. I took advantage of my position vis-à-vis Ms Isaacs. It was wrong, and I regret it. Is that good enough for you?'

'The question is not whether it is good enough for me, Professor Lurie, the question is whether it is good enough for *you*. Does it reflect your sincere feelings?'

He shakes his head. 'I have said the words for you, now you want more, you want me to demonstrate their sincerity. That is preposterous. That is beyond the scope of the law. I have had enough. Let us go back to playing it by the book. I plead guilty. That is as far as I am prepared to go.'

'Right,' says Mathabane from the chair. 'If there are no more questions for Professor Lurie, I will thank him for attending and excuse him.'

At first they do not recognize him. He is halfway down the stairs before he hears the cry *That's him!* followed by a scuffle of feet.

They catch up with him at the foot of the stairs; one even grabs at his jacket to slow him down.

'Can we talk to you just for a minute, Professor Lurie?' says a voice.

He ignores it, pressing on into the crowded lobby, where people turn to stare at the tall man hurrying from his pursuers.

Someone bars his way. 'Hold it!' she says. He averts his face, stretches out a hand. There is a flash.

A girl circles around him. Her hair, plaited with amber beads, hangs straight down on either side of her face. She smiles, showing even white teeth. 'Can we stop and speak?' she says.

'What about?'

A tape recorder is thrust toward him. He pushes it away.

'About how it was,' says the girl.

'How what was?'

The camera flashes again.

'You know, the hearing.'

'I can't comment on that.'

'OK, so what can you comment on?'

'There is nothing I want to comment on.'

The loiterers and the curious have begun to crowd around. If he wants to get away, he will have to push through them.

'Are you sorry?' says the girl. The recorder is thrust closer. 'Do you regret what you did?'

'No,' he says. 'I was enriched by the experience.'

The smile remains on the girl's face. 'So would you do it again?'

'I don't think I will have another chance.'

'But if you had a chance?'

'That isn't a real question.'

She wants more, more words for the belly of the little machine, but for the moment is at a loss for how to suck him into further indiscretion.

'He was what by the experience?' he hears someone ask *sotto voce*.

'He was enriched.'

There is a titter.

'Ask him if he apologized,' someone calls to the girl.

'I already asked.'

Confessions, apologies: why this thirst for abasement? A hush falls. They circle around him like hunters who have cornered a strange beast and do not know how to finish it off.

The photograph appears in the next day's student newspaper, above the caption 'Who's the Dunce Now?' It shows him, eyes cast up to the heavens, reaching out a groping hand toward the camera. The pose is ridiculous enough in itself, but what makes the picture a gem is the inverted waste-paper basket that a young man, grinning broadly, holds above him. By a trick of perspective the basket appears to sit on his head like a dunce's hat. Against such an image, what chance has he?

'Committee tight-lipped on verdict,' reads the headline. 'The disciplinary committee investigating charges of harassment and misconduct against Communications Professor David Lurie was tight-lipped yesterday on its verdict. Chair Manas Mathabane would say only that its findings have been forwarded to the Rector for action.

'Sparring verbally with members of WAR after the hearing, Lurie (53) said he had found his experiences with women students "enriching".

'Trouble first erupted when complaints against Lurie, an expert on romantic poetry, were filed by students in his classes.'

He has a call at home from Mathabane. 'The committee has passed on its recommendation, David, and the Rector has asked me to get back to you one last time. He is prepared not to take extreme measures, he says, on condition that you issue a statement in your own person which will be satisfactory from our point of view as well as yours.'

'Manas, we have been over that ground. I – '

'Wait. Hear me out. I have a draft statement before me which would satisfy our requirements. It is quite short. May I read it to you?'

'Read it.'

Mathabane reads: 'I acknowledge without reservation serious abuses of the human rights of the complainant, as well as abuse of the authority delegated to me by the University. I sincerely apologize to both parties and accept whatever appropriate penalty may be imposed.'

'"Whatever appropriate penalty": what does that mean?'

'My understanding is, you will not be dismissed. In all probability, you will be requested to take a leave of absence. Whether you eventually return to teaching duties will depend on yourself, and on the decision of your Dean and head of department.'

'That is it? That is the package?'

'That is my understanding. If you signify that you subscribe to the statement, which will have the status of a plea in mitigation, the Rector will be prepared to accept it in that spirit.'

'In what spirit?'

'A spirit of repentance.'

'Manas, we went through the repentance business yesterday. I told you what I thought. I won't do it. I appeared before an officially constituted tribunal, before a branch of the law. Before that secular tribunal I pleaded guilty, a secular plea. That plea should suffice. Repentance is neither here nor there. Repentance belongs to another world, to another universe of discourse.'

'You are confusing issues, David. You are not being instructed to repent. What goes on in your soul is dark to us, as members of what you call a secular tribunal if not as fellow human beings. You are being asked to issue a statement.'

'I am being asked to issue an apology about which I may not be sincere?'

'The criterion is not whether you are sincere. That is a matter, as I say, for your own conscience. The criterion is whether you are prepared to acknowledge your fault in a public manner and take steps to remedy it.'

'Now we are truly splitting hairs. You charged me, and I pleaded guilty to the charges. That is all you need from me.'

'No. We want more. Not a great deal more, but more. I hope you can see your way clear to giving us that.'

'Sorry, I can't.'

'David, I can't go on protecting you from yourself. I am tired of it, and so is the rest of the committee. Do you want time to rethink?'

'No.'

'Very well. Then I can only say, you will be hearing from the Rector.'

SEVEN

ONCE HE HAS made up his mind to leave, there is little to hold him back. He clears out the refrigerator, locks up the house, and at noon is on the freeway. A stopover in Oudtshoorn, a crack-of-dawn departure: by mid-morning he is nearing his destination, the town of Salem on the Grahamstown–Kenton road in the Eastern Cape.

His daughter's smallholding is at the end of a winding dirt track some miles outside the town: five hectares of land, most of it arable, a wind-pump, stables and outbuildings, and a low, sprawling farmhouse painted yellow, with a galvanized-iron roof and a covered stoep. The front boundary is marked by a wire fence and clumps of nasturtiums and geraniums; the rest of the front is dust and gravel.

There is an old VW kombi parked in the driveway; he pulls up behind it. From the shade of the stoep Lucy emerges into the sunlight. For a moment he does not recognise her. A year has passed, and she has put on weight. Her hips and breasts are now (he searches for the best word) ample. Comfortably barefoot, she comes to greet him, holding her arms wide, embracing him, kissing him on the cheek.

What a nice girl, he thinks, hugging her; what a nice welcome at the end of a long trip!

The house, which is large, dark, and, even at midday, chilly, dates from the time of large families, of guests by the wagonful. Six years ago Lucy moved in as a member of a commune, a tribe of young people who peddled leather goods and sunbaked pottery in Grahamstown and, in between stands of mealies, grew dagga. When the commune broke up, the rump moving on to New Bethesda, Lucy stayed behind on the smallholding with her friend Helen. She had fallen in love with the place, she said; she wanted to farm it properly. He helped her buy it. Now here she is, flowered dress, bare feet and all, in a house full of the smell of baking, no longer a child playing at farming but a solid countrywoman, a *boervrou*.

'I'm going to put you in Helen's room,' she says. 'It gets the morning sun. You have no idea how cold the mornings have been this winter.'

'How is Helen?' he asks. Helen is a large, sad-looking woman with a deep voice and a bad skin, older than Lucy. He has never been able to understand what Lucy sees in her; privately he wishes Lucy would find, or be found by, someone better.

'Helen has been back in Johannesburg since April. I've been alone, aside from the help.'

'You didn't tell me that. Aren't you nervous by yourself?'

Lucy shrugs. 'There are the dogs. Dogs still mean something. The more dogs, the more deterrence. Anyhow, if there were to be a break-in, I don't see that two people would be better than one.'

'That's very philosophical.'

'Yes. When all else fails, philosophize.'

'But you have a weapon.'

'I have a rifle. I'll show you. I bought it from a neighbour. I haven't ever used it, but I have it.'

'Good. An armed philosopher. I approve.'

Dogs and a gun; bread in the oven and a crop in the earth.

Curious that he and her mother, cityfolk, intellectuals, should have produced this throwback, this sturdy young settler. But perhaps it was not they who produced her: perhaps history had the larger share.

She offers him tea. He is hungry: he wolfs down two blocklike slices of bread with prickly-pear jam, also home-made. He is aware of her eyes on him as he eats. He must be careful: nothing so distasteful to a child as the workings of a parent's body.

Her own fingernails are none too clean. Country dirt: honourable, he supposes.

He unpacks his suitcase in Helen's room. The drawers are empty; in the huge old wardrobe there is only a blue overall hanging. If Helen is away, it is not just for a while.

Lucy takes him on a tour of the premises. She reminds him about not wasting water, about not contaminating the septic tank. He knows the lesson but listens dutifully. Then she shows him over the boarding kennels. On his last visit there had been only one pen. Now there are five, solidly built, with concrete bases, galvanized poles and struts, and heavy-gauge mesh, shaded by young bluegum trees. The dogs are excited to see her: Dobermanns, German Shepherds, ridgebacks, bull terriers, Rottweilers. 'Watchdogs, all of them,' she says. 'Working dogs, on short contracts: two weeks, one week, sometimes just a weekend. The pets tend to come in during the summer holidays.'

'And cats? Don't you take cats?'

'Don't laugh. I'm thinking of branching into cats. I'm just not set up for them yet.'

'Do you still have your stall at the market?'

'Yes, on Saturday mornings. I'll take you along.'

This is how she makes a living: from the kennels, and from selling flowers and garden produce. Nothing could be more simple.

'Don't the dogs get bored?' He points to one, a tan-coloured bulldog bitch with a cage to herself who, head on paws, watches them morosely, not even bothering to get up.

'Katy? She's abandoned. The owners have done a bunk. Account unpaid for months. I don't know what I'm going to do about her. Try to find her a home, I suppose. She's sulking, but otherwise she's all right. She gets taken out every day for exercise. By me or by Petrus. It's part of the package.'

'Petrus?'

'You will meet him. Petrus is my new assistant. In fact, since March, co-proprietor. Quite a fellow.'

He strolls with her past the mud-walled dam, where a family of ducks coasts serenely, past the beehives, and through the garden: flowerbeds and winter vegetables – cauliflowers, potatoes, beetroot, chard, onions. They visit the pump and storage dam on the edge of the property. Rains for the past two years have been good, the water table has risen.

She talks easily about these matters. A frontier farmer of the new breed. In the old days, cattle and maize. Today, dogs and daffodils. The more things change the more they remain the same. History repeating itself, though in a more modest vein. Perhaps history has learned a lesson.

They walk back along an irrigation furrow. Lucy's bare toes grip the red earth, leaving clear prints. A solid woman, embedded in her new life. Good! If this is to be what he leaves behind – this daughter, this woman – then he does not have to be ashamed.

'There's no need to entertain me,' he says, back in the house. 'I've brought my books. I just need a table and chair.'

'Are you working on something in particular?' she asks carefully. His work is not a subject they often talk about.

'I have plans. Something on the last years of Byron. Not a book, or not the kind of book I have written in the past. Something for

62

the stage, rather. Words and music. Characters talking and singing.'

'I didn't know you still had ambitions in that direction.'

'I thought I would indulge myself. But there is more to it than that. One wants to leave something behind. Or at least a man wants to leave something behind. It's easier for a woman.'

'Why is it easier for a woman?'

'Easier, I mean, to produce something with a life of its own.'

'Doesn't being a father count?'

'Being a father . . . I can't help feeling that, by comparison with being a mother, being a father is a rather abstract business. But let us wait and see what comes. If something does come, you will be the first to hear. The first and probably the last.'

'Are you going to write the music yourself?'

'I'll borrow the music, for the most part. I have no qualms about borrowing. At the beginning I thought it was a subject that would call for quite lush orchestration. Like Strauss, say. Which would have been beyond my powers. Now I'm inclining the other way, toward a very meagre accompaniment – violin, cello, oboe or maybe bassoon. But it's all in the realm of ideas as yet. I haven't written a note – I've been distracted. You must have heard about my troubles.'

'Roz mentioned something on the telephone.'

'Well, we won't go into that now. Some other time.'

'Have you left the university for good?'

'I have resigned. I was asked to resign.'

'Will you miss it?'

'Will I miss it? I don't know. I was no great shakes as a teacher. I was having less and less rapport, I found, with my students. What I had to say they didn't care to hear. So perhaps I won't miss it. Perhaps I'll enjoy my release.'

A man is standing in the doorway, a tall man in blue overalls and rubber boots and a woollen cap. 'Petrus, come in, meet my father,' says Lucy.

Petrus wipes his boots. They shake hands. A lined, weathered face; shrewd eyes. Forty? Forty-five?

Petrus turns to Lucy. 'The spray,' he says: 'I have come for the spray.'

'It's in the kombi. Wait here, I'll fetch it.'

He is left with Petrus. 'You look after the dogs,' he says, to break the silence.

'I look after the dogs and I work in the garden. Yes.' Petrus gives a broad smile. 'I am the gardener and the dog-man.' He reflects for a moment. 'The dog-man,' he repeats, savouring the phrase.

'I have just travelled up from Cape Town. There are times when I feel anxious about my daughter all alone here. It is very isolated.'

'Yes,' says Petrus, 'it is dangerous.' He pauses. 'Everything is dangerous today. But here it is all right, I think.' And he gives another smile.

Lucy returns with a small bottle. 'You know the measurement: one teaspoon to ten litres of water.'

'Yes, I know.' And Petrus ducks out through the low doorway.

'Petrus seems a good man,' he remarks.

'He has his head screwed on right.'

'Does he live on the property?'

'He and his wife have the old stable. I've put in electricity. It's quite comfortable. He has another wife in Adelaide, and children, some of them grown up. He goes off and spends time there occasionally.'

He leaves Lucy to her tasks and takes a stroll as far as the Kenton road. A cool winter's day, the sun already dipping over red hills dotted with sparse, bleached grass. Poor land, poor soil, he thinks. Exhausted. Good only for goats. Does Lucy really intend to spend her life here? He hopes it is only a phase.

64

A group of children pass him on their way home from school. He greets them; they greet him back. Country ways. Already Cape Town is receding into the past.

Without warning a memory of the girl comes back: of her neat little breasts with their upstanding nipples, of her smooth flat belly. A ripple of desire passes through him. Evidently whatever it was is not over yet.

He returns to the house and finishes unpacking. A long time since he last lived with a woman. He will have to mind his manners; he will have to be neat.

Ample is a kind word for Lucy. Soon she will be positively heavy. Letting herself go, as happens when one withdraws from the field of love. *Qu'est devenu ce front poli, ces cheveux blonds, sourcils voûtés?*

Supper is simple: soup and bread, then sweet potatoes. Usually he does not like sweet potatoes, but Lucy does something with lemon peel and butter and allspice that makes them palatable, more than palatable.

'Will you be staying a while?' she asks.

'A week? Shall we say a week? Will you be able to bear me that long?'

'You can stay as long as you like. I'm just afraid you'll get bored.'

'I won't be bored.'

'And after the week, where will you go?'

'I don't know yet. Perhaps I'll just go on a ramble, a long ramble.'

'Well, you're welcome to stay.'

'It's nice of you to say so, my dear, but I'd like to keep your friendship. Long visits don't make for good friends.'

'What if we don't call it a visit? What if we call it refuge? Would you accept refuge on an indefinite basis?'

65

'You mean asylum? It's not as bad as that, Lucy. I'm not a fugitive.'

'Roz said the atmosphere was nasty.'

'I brought it on myself. I was offered a compromise, which I wouldn't accept.'

'What kind of compromise?'

'Re-education. Reformation of the character. The code-word was *counselling*.'

'And are you so perfect that you can't do with a little counselling?'

'It reminds me too much of Mao's China. Recantation, self-criticism, public apology. I'm old-fashioned, I would prefer simply to be put against a wall and shot. Have done with it.'

'Shot? For having an affair with a student? A bit extreme, don't you think, David? It must go on all the time. It certainly went on when I was a student. If they prosecuted every case the profession would be decimated.'

He shrugs. 'These are puritanical times. Private life is public business. Prurience is respectable, prurience and sentiment. They wanted a spectacle: breast-beating, remorse, tears if possible. A TV show, in fact. I wouldn't oblige.'

He was going to add, 'The truth is, they wanted me castrated,' but he cannot say the words, not to his daughter. In fact, now that he hears it through another's ears, his whole tirade sounds melodramatic, excessive.

'So you stood your ground and they stood theirs. Is that how it was?'

'More or less.'

'You shouldn't be so unbending, David. It isn't heroic to be unbending. Is there still time to reconsider?'

'No, the sentence is final.'

'No appeal?'

'No appeal. I am not complaining. One can't plead guilty to charges of turpitude and expect a flood of sympathy in return. Not after a certain age. After a certain age one is simply no longer appealing, and that's that. One just has to buckle down and live out the rest of one's life. Serve one's time.'

'Well, that's a pity. Stay here as long as you like. On whatever grounds.'

He goes to bed early. In the middle of the night he is woken by a flurry of barking. One dog in particular barks insistently, mechanically, without cease; the others join in, quiet down, then, loth to admit defeat, join in again.

'Does that go on every night?' he says to Lucy in the morning.

'One gets used to it. I'm sorry.'

He shakes his head.

EIGHT

HE HAS FORGOTTEN how cold winter mornings can be in the uplands of the Eastern Cape. He has not brought the right clothes: he has to borrow a sweater from Lucy.

Hands in pockets, he wanders among the flowerbeds. Out of sight on the Kenton road a car roars past, the sound lingering on the still air. Geese fly in echelon high overhead. What is he going to do with his time?

'Would you like to go for a walk?' says Lucy behind him.

They take three of the dogs along: two young Dobermanns, whom Lucy keeps on a leash, and the bulldog bitch, the abandoned one.

Pinning her ears back, the bitch tries to defecate. Nothing comes.

'She is having problems,' says Lucy. 'I'll have to dose her.'

The bitch continues to strain, hanging her tongue out, glancing around shiftily as if ashamed to be watched.

They leave the road, walk through scrubland, then through sparse pine forest.

'The girl you were involved with,' says Lucy — 'was it serious?'

'Didn't Rosalind tell you the story?'

'Not in any detail.'

'She came from this part of the world. From George. She was

68

in one of my classes. Only middling as a student, but very attractive. Was it serious? I don't know. It certainly had serious consequences.'

'But it's over with now? You're not still hankering after her?'

Is it over with? Does he hanker yet? 'Our contact has ceased,' he says.

'Why did she denounce you?'

'She didn't say; I didn't have a chance to ask. She was in a difficult position. There was a young man, a lover or ex-lover, bullying her. There were the strains of the classroom. And then her parents got to hear and descended on Cape Town. The pressure became too much, I suppose.'

'And there was you.'

'Yes, there was me. I don't suppose I was easy.'

They have arrived at a gate with a sign that says 'SAPPI Industries – Trespassers will be Prosecuted'. They turn.

'Well,' says Lucy, 'you have paid your price. Perhaps, looking back, she won't think too harshly of you. Women can be surprisingly forgiving.'

There is silence. Is Lucy, his child, presuming to tell him about women?

'Have you thought of getting married again?' asks Lucy.

'To someone of my own generation, do you mean? I wasn't made for marriage, Lucy. You have seen that for yourself.'

'Yes. But – '

'But what? But it is unseemly to go on preying on children?'

'I didn't mean that. Just that you are going to find it more difficult, not easier, as time passes.'

Never before have he and Lucy spoken about his intimate life. It is not proving easy. But if not to her, then to whom can he speak?

'Do you remember Blake?' he says. 'Sooner murder an infant in its cradle than nurse unacted desires'?

'Why do you quote that to me?'

'Unacted desires can turn as ugly in the old as in the young.'

'Therefore?'

'Every woman I have been close to has taught me something about myself. To that extent they have made me a better person.'

'I hope you are not claiming the reverse as well. That knowing you has turned your women into better people.'

He looks at her sharply. She smiles. 'Just joking,' she says.

They return along the tar road. At the turnoff to the smallholding there is a painted sign he has not noticed before: 'CUT FLOWERS. CYCADS,' with an arrow: 'I KM'.

'Cycads?' he says. 'I thought cycads were illegal.'

'It's illegal to dig them up in the wild. I grow them from seed. I'll show you.'

They walk on, the young dogs tugging to be free, the bitch padding behind, panting.

'And you? Is this what you want in life?' He waves a hand toward the garden, toward the house with sunlight glinting from its roof.

'It will do,' replies Lucy quietly.

It is Saturday, market day. Lucy wakes him at five, as arranged, with coffee. Swaddled against the cold, they join Petrus in the garden, where by the light of a halogen lamp he is already cutting flowers.

He offers to take over from Petrus, but his fingers are soon so cold that he cannot tie the bunches. He passes the twine back to Petrus and instead wraps and packs.

By seven, with dawn touching the hills and the dogs beginning to stir, the job is done. The kombi is loaded with boxes of flowers, pockets of potatoes, onions, cabbage. Lucy drives, Petrus stays behind. The heater does not work; peering through the misted windscreen, she takes the Grahamstown road. He sits beside her, eating the sandwiches she has made. His nose drips; he hopes she does not notice.

So: a new adventure. His daughter, whom once upon a time he used to drive to school and ballet class, to the circus and the skating rink, is taking him on an outing, showing him life, showing him this other, unfamiliar world.

On Donkin Square stallholders are already setting up trestle tables and laying out their wares. There is a smell of burning meat. A cold mist hangs over the town; people rub their hands, stamp their feet, curse. There is a show of bonhomie from which Lucy, to his relief, holds herself apart.

They are in what appears to be the produce quarter. On their left are three African women with milk, *masa*, butter to sell; also, from a bucket with a wet cloth over it, soup-bones. On their right are an old Afrikaner couple whom Lucy greets as Tante Miems and Oom Koos, and a little assistant in a balaclava cap who cannot be more than ten. Like Lucy, they have potatoes and onions to sell, but also bottled jams, preserves, dried fruit, packets of buchu tea, honeybush tea, herbs.

Lucy has brought two canvas stools. They drink coffee from a thermos flask, waiting for the first customers.

Two weeks ago he was in a classroom explaining to the bored youth of the country the distinction between *drink* and *drink up*, *burned* and *burnt*. The perfective, signifying an action carried through to its conclusion. How far away it all seems! I live, I have lived, I lived.

Lucy's potatoes, tumbled out into a bushel basket, have been washed clean. Koos and Miems's are still speckled with earth. In the course of the morning Lucy takes in nearly five hundred rand. Her flowers sell steadily; at eleven o'clock she drops her prices and the last of the produce goes. There is plenty of trade too at the milk-and-meat stall; but the old couple, seated side by side wooden and unsmiling, do less well.

Many of Lucy's customers know her by name: middle-aged women, most of them, with a touch of the proprietary in their attitude to her, as though her success were theirs too. Each time she introduces him: 'Meet my father, David Lurie, on a visit from Cape Town.' 'You must be proud of your daughter, Mr Lurie,' they say. 'Yes, very proud,' he replies.

'Bev runs the animal refuge,' says Lucy, after one of the introductions. 'I give her a hand sometimes. We'll drop in at her place on the way back, if that is all right with you.'

He has not taken to Bev Shaw, a dumpy, bustling little woman with black freckles, close-cropped, wiry hair, and no neck. He does not like women who make no effort to be attractive. It is a resistance he has had to Lucy's friends before. Nothing to be proud of: a prejudice that has settled in his mind, settled down. His mind has become a refuge for old thoughts, idle, indigent, with nowhere else to go. He ought to chase them out, sweep the premises clean. But he does not care to do so, or does not care enough.

The Animal Welfare League, once an active charity in Grahamstown, has had to close down its operation. However, a handful of volunteers led by Bev Shaw still runs a clinic from the old premises.

He has nothing against the animal lovers with whom Lucy has been mixed up as long as he can remember. The world would no doubt be a worse place without them. So when Bev Shaw opens her front door he puts on a good face, though in fact he is repelled by the odours of cat urine and dog mange and Jeyes Fluid that greet them.

The house is just as he had imagined it would be: rubbishy furniture, a clutter of ornaments (porcelain shepherdesses, cowbells, an ostrich-feather flywhisk), the yammer of a radio, the cheeping of birds in cages, cats everywhere underfoot. There is not only Bev Shaw, there is Bill Shaw too, equally squat, drinking tea at the kitchen table, with a beet-red face and silver hair and a sweater with a floppy collar. 'Sit down, sit down, Dave,' says Bill. 'Have a cup, make yourself at home.'

It has been a long morning, he is tired, the last thing he wants to do is trade small talk with these people. He casts Lucy a glance. 'We won't stay, Bill,' she says, 'I'm just picking up some medicines.'

Through a window he glimpses the Shaws' back yard: an apple tree dropping wormridden fruit, rampant weeds, an area fenced in with galvanized-iron sheets, wooden pallets, old tyres, where chickens scratch around and what looks uncommonly like a duiker snoozes in a corner.

'What do you think?' says Lucy afterwards in the car.

'I don't want to be rude. It's a subculture of its own, I'm sure. Don't they have children?'

'No, no children. Don't underestimate Bev. She's not a fool. She does an enormous amount of good. She's been going into D Village for years, first for Animal Welfare, now on her own.'

'It must be a losing battle.'

'Yes, it is. There is no funding any longer. On the list of the nation's priorities, animals come nowhere.'

'She must get despondent. You too.'

'Yes. No. Does it matter? The animals she helps aren't despondent. They are greatly relieved.'

'That's wonderful, then. I'm sorry, my child, I just find it hard to whip up an interest in the subject. It's admirable, what you do, what she does, but to me animal-welfare people are a bit like Christians of a certain kind. Everyone is so cheerful and well-intentioned that after a while you itch to go off and do some raping and pillaging. Or to kick a cat.'

73

He is surprised by his outburst. He is not in a bad temper, not in the least.

'You think I ought to involve myself in more important things,' says Lucy. They are on the open road; she drives without glancing at him. 'You think, because I am your daughter, I ought to be doing something better with my life.'

He is already shaking his head. 'No . . . no . . . no,' he murmurs.

'You think I ought to be painting still lives or teaching myself Russian. You don't approve of friends like Bev and Bill Shaw because they are not going to lead me to a higher life.'

'That's not true, Lucy.'

'But it is true. They are not going to lead me to a higher life, and the reason is, there is no higher life. This is the only life there is. Which we share with animals. That's the example that people like Bev try to set. That's the example I try to follow. To share some of our human privilege with the beasts. I don't want to come back in another existence as a dog or a pig and have to live as dogs or pigs live under us.'

'Lucy, my dearest, don't be cross. Yes, I agree, this is the only life there is. As for animals, by all means let us be kind to them. But let us not lose perspective. We are of a different order of creation from the animals. Not higher, necessarily, just different. So if we are going to be kind, let it be out of simple generosity, not because we feel guilty or fear retribution.'

Lucy draws a breath. She seems about to respond to his homily, but then does not. They arrive at the house in silence.

NINE

HE IS SITTING in the front room, watching soccer on television. The score is nil-all; neither team seems interested in winning.

The commentary alternates between Sotho and Xhosa, languages of which he understands not a word. He turns the sound down to a murmur. Saturday afternoon in South Africa: a time consecrated to men and their pleasures. He nods off.

When he awakes, Petrus is beside him on the sofa with a bottle of beer in his hand. He has turned the volume higher.

'Bushbucks,' says Petrus. 'My team. Bushbucks and Sundowns.'

Sundowns take a corner. There is a mêlée in the goalmouth. Petrus groans and clasps his head. When the dust clears, the Bushbucks goalkeeper is lying on the ground with the ball under his chest. 'He is good! He is good!' says Petrus. 'He is a good goalkeeper. They must keep him.'

The game ends scoreless. Petrus switches channels. Boxing: two tiny men, so tiny that they barely come up to the referee's chest, circle, leap in, belabour each other.

He gets up, wanders through to the back of the house. Lucy is lying on her bed, reading. 'What are you reading?' he says. She looks at him quizzically, then takes the earplugs out of her ears.

75

'What are you reading?' he repeats; and then, 'It's not working out, is it? Shall I leave?'

She smiles, lays her book aside. *The Mystery of Edwin Drood*: not what he would have expected. 'Sit down,' she says.

He sits on the bed, idly fondles her bare foot. A good foot, shapely. Good bones, like her mother. A woman in the flower of her years, attractive despite the heaviness, despite the unflattering clothes.

'From my point of view, David, it is working out perfectly well. I'm glad to have you here. It takes a while to adjust to the pace of country life, that's all. Once you find things to do you won't be so bored.'

He nods absentmindedly. Attractive, he is thinking, yet lost to men. Need he reproach himself, or would it have worked out like that anyway? From the day his daughter was born he has felt for her nothing but the most spontaneous, most unstinting love. Impossible she has been unaware of it. Has it been too much, that love? Has she found it a burden? Has it pressed down on her? Has she given it a darker reading?

He wonders how it is for Lucy with her lovers, how it is for her lovers with her. He has never been afraid to follow a thought down its winding track, and he is not afraid now. Has he fathered a woman of passion? What can she draw on, what not, in the realm of the senses? Are he and she capable of talking about that too? Lucy has not led a protected life. Why should they not be open with each other, why should they draw lines, in times when no one else does?

'Once I find things to do,' he says, coming back from his wanderings. 'What do you suggest?'

'You could help with the dogs. You could cut up the dog-meat. I've always found that difficult. Then there is Petrus. Petrus is busy establishing his own lands. You could give him a hand.'

'Give Petrus a hand. I like that. I like the historical piquancy. Will he pay me a wage for my labour, do you think?'

'Ask him. I'm sure he will. He got a Land Affairs grant earlier this year, enough to buy a hectare and a bit from me. I didn't tell you? The boundary line goes through the dam. We share the dam. Everything from there to the fence is his. He has a cow that will calve in the spring. He has two wives, or a wife and a girlfriend. If he has played his cards right he could get a second grant to put up a house; then he can move out of the stable. By Eastern Cape standards he is a man of substance. Ask him to pay you. He can afford it. I'm not sure I can afford him any more.'

'All right, I'll handle the dog-meat, I'll offer to dig for Petrus. What else?'

'You can help at the clinic. They are desperate for volunteers.'

'You mean help Bev Shaw.'

'Yes.'

'I don't think she and I will hit it off.'

'You don't need to hit it off with her. You have only to help her. But don't expect to be paid. You will have to do it out of the goodness of your heart.'

'I'm dubious, Lucy. It sounds suspiciously like community service. It sounds like someone trying to make reparation for past misdeeds.'

'As to your motives, David, I can assure you, the animals at the clinic won't query them. They won't ask and they won't care.'

'All right, I'll do it. But only as long as I don't have to become a better person. I am not prepared to be reformed. I want to go on being myself. I'll do it on that basis.' His hand still rests on her foot; now he grips her ankle tight. 'Understood?'

She gives him what he can only call a sweet smile. 'So you are determined to go on being bad. Mad, bad, and dangerous to know. I promise, no one will ask you to change.'

She teases him as her mother used to tease him. Her wit, if anything, sharper. He has always been drawn to women of wit. Wit and beauty. With the best will in the world he could not find wit in Meláni. But plenty of beauty.

Again it runs through him: a light shudder of voluptuousness. He is aware of Lucy observing him. He does not appear to be able to conceal it. Interesting.

He gets up, goes out into the yard. The younger dogs are delighted to see him: they trot back and forth in their cages, whining eagerly. But the old bulldog bitch barely stirs.

He enters her cage, closes the door behind him. She raises her head, regards him, lets her head fall again; her old dugs hang slack.

He squats down, tickles her behind the ears. 'Abandoned, are we?' he murmurs.

He stretches out beside her on the bare concrete. Above is the pale blue sky. His limbs relax.

This is how Lucy finds him. He must have fallen asleep: the first he knows, she is in the cage with the water-can, and the bitch is up, sniffing her feet.

'Making friends?' says Lucy.

'She's not easy to make friends with.'

'Poor old Katy, she's in mourning. No one wants her, and she knows it. The irony is, she must have offspring all over the district who would be happy to share their homes with her. But it's not in their power to invite her. They are part of the furniture, part of the alarm system. They do us the honour of treating us like gods, and we respond by treating them like things.'

They leave the cage. The bitch slumps down, closes her eyes.

'The Church Fathers had a long debate about them, and decided they don't have proper souls,' he observes. 'Their souls are tied to their bodies and die with them.'

Lucy shrugs. 'I'm not sure that I have a soul. I wouldn't know a soul if I saw one.'

'That's not true. You are a soul. We are all souls. We are souls before we are born.'

She regards him oddly.

'What will you do with her?' he says.

'With Katy? I'll keep her, if it comes to that.'

'Don't you ever put animals down?'

'No, I don't. Bev does. It is a job no one else wants to do, so she has taken it upon herself. It cuts her up terribly. You underestimate her. She is a more interesting person than you think. Even in your own terms.'

His own terms: what are they? That dumpy little women with ugly voices deserve to be ignored? A shadow of grief falls over him: for Katy, alone in her cage, for himself, for everyone. He sighs deeply, not stifling the sigh. 'Forgive me, Lucy,' he says.

'Forgive you? For what?' She is smiling lightly, mockingly.

'For being one of the two mortals assigned to usher you into the world and for not turning out to be a better guide. But I'll go and help Bev Shaw. Provided that I don't have to call her Bev. It's a silly name to go by. It reminds me of cattle. When shall I start?'

'I'll give her a call.'

TEN

THE SIGN OUTSIDE the clinic reads ANIMAL WELFARE LEAGUE W.O. 1529. Below is a line stating the daily hours, but this has been taped over. At the door is a line of waiting people, some with animals. As soon as he gets out of his car there are children all around him, begging for money or just staring. He makes his way through the crush, and through a sudden cacophony as two dogs, held back by their owners, snarl and snap at each other.

The small, bare waiting-room is packed. He has to step over someone's legs to get in.

'Mrs Shaw?' he inquires.

An old woman nods toward a doorway closed off with a plastic curtain. The woman holds a goat on a short rope; it glares nervously, eyeing the dogs, its hooves clicking on the hard floor.

In the inner room, which smells pungently of urine, Bev Shaw is working at a low steel-topped table. With a pencil-light she is peering down the throat of a young dog that looks like a cross between a ridgeback and a jackal. Kneeling on the table a barefoot child, evidently the owner, has the dog's head clamped under his arm and is trying to hold its jaws open. A low, gurgling snarl comes from its throat; its powerful hindquarters strain. Awkwardly he joins in the tussle, pressing the dog's hind legs together, forcing it to sit on its haunches.

'Thank you,' says Bev Shaw. Her face is flushed. 'There's an abscess here from an impacted tooth. We have no antibiotics, so – hold him still, *boytjie!* – so we'll just have to lance it and hope for the best.'

She probes inside the mouth with a lancet. The dog gives a tremendous jerk, breaks free of him, almost breaks free of the boy. He grasps it as it scrabbles to get off the table; for a moment its eyes, full of rage and fear, glare into his.

'On his side – so,' says Bev Shaw. Making crooning noises, she expertly trips up the dog and turns it on its side. 'The belt,' she says. He passes a belt around its body and she buckles it. 'So,' says Bev Shaw. 'Think comforting thoughts, think strong thoughts. They can smell what you are thinking.'

He leans his full weight on the dog. Gingerly, one hand wrapped in an old rag, the child prises open the jaws again. The dog's eyes roll in terror. They can smell what you are thinking: what nonsense! 'There, there!' he murmurs. Bev Shaw probes again with the lancet. The dog gags, goes rigid, then relaxes.

'So,' she says, 'now we must let nature take her course.' She unbuckles the belt, speaks to the child in what sounds like very halting Xhosa. The dog, on its feet, cowers under the table. There is a spattering of blood and saliva on the surface; Bev wipes it off. The child coaxes the dog out.

'Thank you, Mr Lurie. You have a good presence. I sense that you like animals.'

'Do I like animals? I eat them, so I suppose I must like them, some parts of them.'

Her hair is a mass of little curls. Does she make the curls herself, with tongs? Unlikely: it would take hours every day. They must grow that way. He has never seen such a *tessitura* from close by. The veins on her ears are visible as a filigree of red and purple. The veins of her nose too. And then a chin that comes straight out of her chest, like a pouter pigeon's. As an ensemble, remarkably unattractive.

She is pondering his words, whose tone she appears to have missed.

'Yes, we eat up a lot of animals in this country,' she says. 'It doesn't seem to do us much good. I'm not sure how we will justify it to them.' Then: 'Shall we start on the next one?'

Justify it? When? At the Great Reckoning? He would be curious to hear more, but this is not the time.

The goat, a fullgrown buck, can barely walk. One half of his scrotum, yellow and purple, is swollen like a balloon; the other half is a mass of caked blood and dirt. He has been savaged by dogs, the old woman says. But he seems bright enough, cheery, combative. While Bev Shaw is examining him, he passes a short burst of pellets on to the floor. Standing at his head, gripping his horns, the woman pretends to reprove him.

Bev Shaw touches the scrotum with a swab. The goat kicks. 'Can you fasten his legs?' she asks, and indicates how. He straps the right hind leg to the right foreleg. The goat tries to kick again, teeters. She swabs the wound gently. The goat trembles, gives a bleat: an ugly sound, low and hoarse.

As the dirt comes away, he sees that the wound is alive with white grubs waving their blind heads in the air. He shudders. 'Blowfly,' says Bev Shaw. 'At least a week old.' She purses her lips. 'You should have brought him in long ago,' she says to the woman. 'Yes,' says the woman. 'Every night the dogs come. It is too, too bad. Five hundred rand you pay for a man like him.'

Bev Shaw straightens up. 'I don't know what we can do. I don't have the experience to try a removal. She can wait for Dr Oosthuizen on Thursday, but the old fellow will come out sterile anyway, and does she want that? And then there is the question of antibiotics. Is she prepared to spend money on antibiotics?'

She kneels down again beside the goat, nuzzles his throat, stroking the throat upward with her own hair. The goat trembles but is still. She motions to the woman to let go of the horns. The woman obeys. The goat does not stir.

She is whispering. 'What do you say, my friend?' he hears her say. 'What do you say? Is it enough?'

The goat stands stock still as if hypnotized. Bev Shaw continues to stroke him with her head. She seems to have lapsed into a trance of her own.

She collects herself and gets to her feet. 'I'm afraid it's too late,' she says to the woman. 'I can't make him better. You can wait for the doctor on Thursday, or you can leave him with me. I can give him a quiet end. He will let me do that for him. Shall I? Shall I keep him here?'

The woman wavers, then shakes her head. She begins to tug the goat toward the door.

'You can have him back afterwards,' says Bev Shaw. 'I will help him through, that's all.' Though she tries to control her voice, he can hear the accents of defeat. The goat hears them too: he kicks against the strap, bucking and plunging, the obscene bulge quivering behind him. The woman drags the strap loose, casts it aside. Then they are gone.

'What was that all about?' he asks.

Bev Shaw hides her face, blows her nose. 'It's nothing. I keep enough lethal for bad cases, but we can't force the owners. It's their animal, they like to slaughter in their own way. What a pity! Such a good old fellow, so brave and straight and confident!'

Lethal: the name of a drug? He would not put it beyond the drug companies. Sudden darkness, from the waters of Lethe.

'Perhaps he understands more than you guess,' he says. To his own surprise, he is trying to comfort her. 'Perhaps he has already been through it. Born with foreknowledge, so to speak. This is

Africa, after all. There have been goats here since the beginning of time. They don't have to be told what steel is for, and fire. They know how death comes to a goat. They are born prepared.'

'Do you think so?' she says. 'I'm not sure. I don't think we are ready to die, any of us, not without being escorted.'

Things are beginning to fall into place. He has a first inkling of the task this ugly little woman has set herself. This bleak building is a place not of healing – her doctoring is too amateurish for that – but of last resort. He recalls the story of – who was it? St Hubert? – who gave refuge to a deer that clattered into his chapel, panting and distraught, fleeing the huntsmen's dogs. Bev Shaw, not a veterinarian but a priestess, full of New Age mumbo jumbo, trying, absurdly, to lighten the load of Africa's suffering beasts. Lucy thought he would find her interesting. But Lucy is wrong. Interesting is not the word.

He spends all afternoon in the surgery, helping as far as he is able. When the last of the day's cases has been dealt with, Bev Shaw shows him around the yard. In the avian cage there is only one bird, a young fish-eagle with a splinted wing. For the rest there are dogs: not Lucy's well-groomed thoroughbreds but a mob of scrawny mongrels filling two pens to bursting point, barking, yapping, whining, leaping with excitement.

He helps her pour out dry food and fill the water-troughs. They empty two ten-kilogram bags.

'How do you pay for this stuff?' he asks.

'We get it wholesale. We hold public collections. We get donations. We offer a free neutering service, and get a grant for that.'

'Who does the neutering?

'Dr Oosthuizen, our vet. But he comes in only one afternoon a week.'

He is watching the dogs eat. It surprises him how little fighting there is. The small, the weak hold back, accepting their lot, waiting their turn.

'The trouble is, there are just too many of them,' says Bev Shaw. 'They don't understand it, of course, and we have no way of telling them. Too many by our standards, not by theirs. They would just multiply and multiply if they had their way, until they filled the earth. They don't think it's a bad thing to have lots of offspring. The more the jollier. Cats the same.'

'And rats.'

'And rats. Which reminds me: check yourself for fleas when you get home.'

One of the dogs, replete, eyes shining with wellbeing, sniffs his fingers through the mesh, licks them.

'They are very egalitarian, aren't they,' he remarks. 'No classes. No one too high and mighty to smell another's backside.' He squats, allows the dog to smell his face, his breath. It has what he thinks of as an intelligent look, though it is probably nothing of the kind. 'Are they all going to die?'

'Those that no one wants. We'll put them down.'

'And you are the one who does the job.'

'Yes.'

'You don't mind?'

'I do mind. I mind deeply. I wouldn't want someone doing it for me who didn't mind. Would you?'

He is silent. Then: 'Do you know why my daughter sent me to you?'

'She told me you were in trouble.'

'Not just in trouble. In what I suppose one would call disgrace.'

He watches her closely. She seems uncomfortable; but perhaps he is imagining it.

'Knowing that, do you still have a use for me?' he says.

'If you are prepared . . .' She opens her hands, presses them together, opens them again. She does not know what to say, and he does not help her.

He has stayed with his daughter only for brief periods before. Now he is sharing her house, her life. He has to be careful not to allow old habits to creep back, the habits of a parent: putting the toilet roll on the spool, switching off lights, chasing the cat off the sofa. Practise for old age, he admonishes himself. Practise fitting in. Practise for the old folks' home.

He pretends he is tired and, after supper, withdraws to his room, where faintly the sounds come to him of Lucy leading her own life: drawers opening and shutting, the radio, the murmur of a telephone conversation. Is she calling Johannesburg, speaking to Helen? Is his presence here keeping the two of them apart? Would they dare to share a bed while he was in the house? If the bed creaked in the night, would they be embarrassed? Embarrassed enough to stop? But what does he know about what women do together? Maybe women do not need to make beds creak. And what does he know about these two in particular, Lucy and Helen? Perhaps they sleep together merely as children do, cuddling, touching, giggling, reliving girlhood — sisters more than lovers. Sharing a bed, sharing a bathtub, baking gingerbread cookies, trying on each other's clothes. Sapphic love: an excuse for putting on weight.

The truth is, he does not like to think of his daughter in the throes of passion with another woman, and a plain one at that. Yet would he be any happier if the lover were a man? What does he really want for Lucy? Not that she should be forever a child, forever innocent, forever his — certainly not that. But he is a father, that is his fate, and as a father grows older he turns more and more — it cannot be helped — toward his daughter. She becomes his second salvation, the bride of his youth reborn. No wonder, in fairy-stories, queens try to hound their daughters to their death!

He sighs. Poor Lucy! Poor daughters! What a destiny, what a burden to bear! And sons: they too must have their tribulations, though he knows less about that.

He wishes he could sleep. But he is cold, and not sleepy at all.

He gets up, drapes a jacket over his shoulders, returns to bed. He is reading Byron's letters of 1820. Fat, middle-aged at thirty-two, Byron is living with the Guicciolis in Ravenna: with Teresa, his complacent, short-legged mistress, and her suave, malevolent husband. Summer heat, late-afternoon tea, provincial gossip, yawns barely hidden. 'The women sit in a circle and the men play dreary Faro,' writes Byron. In adultery, all the tedium of marriage rediscovered. 'I have always looked to thirty as the barrier to any real or fierce delight in the passions.'

He sighs again. How brief the summer, before the autumn and then the winter! He reads on past midnight, yet even so cannot get to sleep.

ELEVEN

IT IS WEDNESDAY. He gets up early, but Lucy is up before him. He finds her watching the wild geese on the dam.

'Aren't they lovely,' she says. 'They come back every year. The same three. I feel so lucky to be visited. To be the one chosen.'

Three. That would be a solution of sorts. He and Lucy and Melanie. Or he and Melanie and Soraya.

They have breakfast together, then take the two Dobermanns for a walk.

'Do you think you could live here, in this part of the world?' asks Lucy out of the blue.

'Why? Do you need a new dog-man?'

'No, I wasn't thinking of that. But surely you could get a job at Rhodes University – you must have contacts there – or at Port Elizabeth.'

'I don't think so, Lucy. I'm no longer marketable. The scandal will follow me, stick to me. No, if I took a job it would have to be as something obscure, like a ledger clerk, if they still have them, or a kennel attendant.'

'But if you want to put a stop to the scandal-mongering, shouldn't you be ·standing up for yourself? Doesn't gossip just multiply if you run away?'

As a child Lucy had been quiet and self-effacing, observing him but never, as far as he knew, judging him. Now, in her middle twenties, she has begun to separate. The dogs, the gardening, the astrology books, the asexual clothes: in each he recognizes a statement of independence, considered, purposeful. The turn away from men too. Making her own life. Coming out of his shadow. Good! He approves!

'Is that what you think I have done?' he says. 'Run away from the scene of the crime?'

'Well, you have withdrawn. For practical purposes, what is the difference?'

'You miss the point, my dear. The case you want me to make is a case that can no longer be made, *basta*. Not in our day. If I tried to make it I would not be heard.'

'That's not true. Even if you are what you say, a moral dinosaur, there is a curiosity to hear the dinosaur speak. I for one am curious. What is your case? Let us hear it.'

He hesitates. Does she really want him to trot out more of his intimacies?

'My case rests on the rights of desire,' he says. 'On the god who makes even the small birds quiver.'

He sees himself in the girl's flat, in her bedroom, with the rain pouring down outside and the heater in the corner giving off a smell of paraffin, kneeling over her, peeling off her clothes, while her arms flop like the arms of a dead person. *I was a servant of Eros*: that is what he wants to say, but does he have the effrontery? *It was a god who acted through me*. What vanity! Yet not a lie, not entirely. In the whole wretched business there was something generous that was doing its best to flower. If only he had known the time would be so short!

He tries again, more slowly. 'When you were small, when we were still living in Kenilworth, the people next door had a dog, a golden retriever. I don't know whether you remember.'

89

'Dimly.'

'It was a male. Whenever there was a bitch in the vicinity it would get excited and unmanageable, and with Pavlovian regularity the owners would beat it. This went on until the poor dog didn't know what to do. At the smell of a bitch it would chase around the garden with its ears flat and its tail between its legs, whining, trying to hide.'

He pauses. 'I don't see the point,' says Lucy. And indeed, what is the point?

'There was something so ignoble in the spectacle that I despaired. One can punish a dog, it seems to me, for an offence like chewing a slipper. A dog will accept the justice of that: a beating for a chewing. But desire is another story. No animal will accept the justice of being punished for following its instincts.'

'So males must be allowed to follow their instincts unchecked? Is that the moral?'

'No, that is not the moral. What was ignoble about the Kenilworth spectacle was that the poor dog had begun to hate its own nature. It no longer needed to be beaten. It was ready to punish itself. At that point it would have been better to shoot it.'

'Or to have it fixed.'

'Perhaps. But at the deepest level I think it might have preferred being shot. It might have preferred that to the options it was offered: on the one hand, to deny its nature, on the other, to spend the rest of its days padding about the living-room, sighing and sniffing the cat and getting portly.'

'Have you always felt this way, David?'

'No, not always. Sometimes I have felt just the opposite. That desire is a burden we could well do without.'

'I must say,' says Lucy, 'that is a view I incline toward myself.'

He waits for her to go on, but she does not. 'In any event,' she says, 'to return to the subject, you are safely expelled. Your colleagues can breathe easy again, while the scapegoat wanders in the wilderness.'

A statement? A question? Does she believe he is just a scapegoat?

'I don't think scapegoating is the best description,' he says cautiously. 'Scapegoating worked in practice while it still had religious power behind it. You loaded the sins of the city on to the goat's back and drove it out, and the city was cleansed. It worked because everyone knew how to read the ritual, including the gods. Then the gods died, and all of a sudden you had to cleanse the city without divine help. Real actions were demanded instead of symbolism. The censor was born, in the Roman sense. Watchfulness became the watchword: the watchfulness of all over all. Purgation was replaced by the purge.'

He is getting carried away; he is lecturing. 'Anyway,' he concludes, 'having said farewell to the city, what do I find myself doing in the wilderness? Doctoring dogs. Playing right-hand man to a woman who specializes in sterilization and euthanasia.'

Lucy laughs. 'Bev? You think Bev is part of the repressive apparatus? Bev is in awe of you! You are a professor. She has never met an old-fashioned professor before. She is frightened of making grammar mistakes in front of you.'

Three men are coming toward them on the path, or two men and a boy. They are walking fast, with countrymen's long strides. The dog at Lucy's side slows down, bristles.

'Should we be nervous?' he murmurs.

'I don't know.'

She shortens the Dobermanns' leashes. The men are upon them. A nod, a greeting, and they have passed.

'Who are they?' he asks.

'I've never laid eyes on them before.'

They reach the plantation boundary and turn back. The strangers are out of sight.

As they near the house they hear the caged dogs in an uproar. Lucy quickens her pace.

The three are there, waiting for them. The two men stand at a remove while the boy, beside the cages, hisses at the dogs and makes sudden, threatening gestures. The dogs, in a rage, bark and snap. The dog at Lucy's side tries to tug loose. Even the old bulldog bitch, whom he seems to have adopted as his own, is growling softly.

'Petrus!' calls Lucy. But there is no sign of Petrus. 'Get away from the dogs!' she shouts. *'Hamba!'*

The boy saunters off and rejoins his companions. He has a flat, expressionless face and piggish eyes; he wears a flowered shirt, baggy trousers, a little yellow sunhat. His companions are both in overalls. The taller of them is handsome, strikingly handsome, with a high forehead, sculpted cheekbones, wide, flaring nostrils.

At Lucy's approach the dogs calm down. She opens the third cage and releases the two Dobermanns into it. A brave gesture, he thinks to himself; but is it wise?

To the men she says: 'What do you want?'

The young one speaks. 'We must telephone.'

'Why must you telephone?'

'His sister' – he gestures vaguely behind him – 'is having an accident.'

'An accident?'

'Yes, very bad.'

'What kind of accident?'

'A baby.'

'His sister is having a baby?'

'Yes.'

'Where are you from?'

'From Erasmuskraal.'

He and Lucy exchange glances. Erasmuskraal, inside the forestry concession, is a hamlet with no electricity, no telephone. The story makes sense.

'Why didn't you phone from the forestry station?'

'Is no one there.'

'Stay out here,' Lucy murmurs to him; and then, to the boy: 'Who is it who wants to telephone?'

He indicates the tall, handsome man.

'Come in,' she says. She unlocks the back door and enters. The tall man follows. After a moment the second man pushes past him and enters the house too.

Something is wrong, he knows at once. 'Lucy, come out here!' he calls, unsure for the moment whether to follow or wait where he can keep an eye on the boy.

From the house there is silence. 'Lucy!' he calls again, and is about to go in when the door-latch clicks shut.

'Petrus!' he shouts as loudly as he can.

The boy turns and sprints, heading for the front door. He lets go the bulldog's leash. 'Get him!' he shouts. The dog trots heavily after the boy.

In front of the house he catches up with them. The boy has picked up a bean-stake and is using it to keep the dog at bay. 'Shu . . . shu . . . shu!' he pants, thrusting with the stick. Growling softly, the dog circles left and right.

Abandoning them, he rushes back to the kitchen door. The bottom leaf is not bolted: a few heavy kicks and it swings open. On all fours he creeps into the kitchen.

A blow catches him on the crown of the head. He has time to think, *If I am still conscious then I am all right*, before his limbs turn to water and he crumples.

He is aware of being dragged across the kitchen floor. Then he blacks out.

He is lying face down on cold tiles. He tries to stand up but his legs are somehow blocked from moving. He closes his eyes again

He is in the lavatory, the lavatory of Lucy's house. Dizzily he gets to his feet. The door is locked, the key is gone.

He sits down on the toilet seat and tries to recover. The house is still; the dogs are barking, but more in duty, it seems, than in frenzy.

'Lucy!' he croaks, and then, louder: 'Lucy!'

He tries to kick at the door, but he is not himself, and the space too cramped anyway, the door too old and solid.

So it has come, the day of testing. Without warning, without fanfare, it is here, and he is in the middle of it. In his chest his heart hammers so hard that it too, in its dumb way, must know. How will they stand up to the testing, he and his heart?

His child is in the hands of strangers. In a minute, in an hour, it will be too late; whatever is happening to her will be set in stone, will belong to the past. But *now* it is not too late. *Now* he must do something.

Though he strains to hear, he can make out no sound from the house. Yet if his child were calling, however mutely, surely he would hear!

He batters the door. 'Lucy!' he shouts. 'Lucy! Speak to me!'

The door opens, knocking him off balance. Before him stands the second man, the shorter one, holding an empty one-litre bottle by the neck. 'The keys,' says the man.

'No.'

The man gives him a push. He stumbles back, sits down heavily. The man raises the bottle. His face is placid, without trace of anger. It is merely a job he is doing: getting someone to hand over an article. If it entails hitting him with a bottle, he will hit him, hit him as many times as is necessary, if necessary break the bottle too.

'Take them,' he says. 'Take everything. Just leave my daughter alone.'

94

Without a word the man takes the keys, locks him in again.

He shivers. A dangerous trio. Why did he not recognise it in time? But they are not harming him, not yet. Is it possible that what the house has to offer will be enough for them? Is it possible they will leave Lucy unharmed too?

From behind the house comes the sound of voices. The barking of the dogs grows louder again, more excited. He stands on the toilet seat and peers through the bars of the window.

Carrying Lucy's rifle and a bulging garbage bag, the second man is just disappearing around the corner of the house. A car door slams. He recognizes the sound: his car. The man reappears empty-handed. For a moment the two of them look straight into each other's eyes. 'Hai!' says the man, and smiles grimly, and calls out some words. There is a burst of laughter. A moment later the boy joins him, and they stand beneath the window, inspecting their prisoner, discussing his fate.

He speaks Italian, he speaks French, but Italian and French will not save him here in darkest Africa. He is helpless, an Aunt Sally, a figure from a cartoon, a missionary in cassock and topi waiting with clasped hands and upcast eyes while the savages jaw away in their own lingo preparatory to plunging him into their boiling cauldron. Mission work: what has it left behind, that huge enterprise of upliftment? Nothing that he can see.

Now the tall man appears from around the front, carrying the rifle. With practised ease he brings a cartridge up into the breech, thrusts the muzzle into the dogs' cage. The biggest of the German Shepherds, slavering with rage, snaps at it. There is a heavy report; blood and brains splatter the cage. For a moment the barking ceases. The man fires twice more. One dog, shot through the chest, dies at once; another, with a gaping throat-wound, sits down heavily, flattens its ears, following with its gaze the movements of this being who does not even bother to administer a *coup de grâce*.

A hush falls. The remaining three dogs, with nowhere to hide, retreat to the back of the pen, milling about, whining softly. Taking his time between shots, the man picks them off.

Footfalls along the passage, and the door to the toilet swings open again. The second man stands before him; behind him he glimpses the boy in the flowered shirt, eating from a tub of ice-cream. He tries to shoulder his way out, gets past the man, then falls heavily. Some kind of trip: they must practise it in soccer.

As he lies sprawled he is splashed from head to foot with liquid. His eyes burn, he tries to wipe them. He recognizes the smell: methylated spirits. Struggling to get up, he is pushed back into the lavatory. The scrape of a match, and at once he is bathed in cool blue flame.

So he was wrong! He and his daughter are not being let off lightly after all! He can burn, he can die; and if he can die, then so can Lucy, above all Lucy!

He strikes at his face like a madman; his hair crackles as it catches alight; he throws himself about, hurling out shapeless bellows that have no words behind them, only fear. He tries to stand up and is forced down again. For a moment his vision clears and he sees, inches from his face, blue overalls and a shoe. The toe of the shoe curls upward; there are blades of grass sticking out from the tread.

A flame dances soundlessly on the back of his hand. He struggles to his knees and plunges the hand into the toilet bowl. Behind him the door closes and the key turns.

He hangs over the toilet bowl, splashing water over his face, dousing his head. There is a nasty smell of singed hair. He stands up, beats out the last of the flames on his clothes.

With wads of wet paper he bathes his face. His eyes are stinging, one eyelid is already closing. He runs a hand over his head and his fingertips come away black with soot. Save for a patch over one ear, he seems to have no hair; his whole scalp is tender. Everything is tender, everything is burned. Burned, burnt.

'Lucy!' he shouts. 'Are you here?'

A vision comes to him of Lucy struggling with the two in the blue overalls, struggling against them. He writhes, trying to blank it out.

He hears his car start, and the crunch of tyres on gravel. Is it over? Are they, unbelievably, going?

'Lucy!' he shouts, over and over, till he can hear an edge of craziness in his voice.

At last, blessedly, the key turns in the lock. By the time he has the door open, Lucy has turned her back on him. She is wearing a bathrobe, her feet are bare, her hair wet.

He trails after her through the kitchen, where the refrigerator stands open and food lies scattered all over the floor. She stands at the back door taking in the carnage of the dog-pens. 'My darlings, my darlings!' he hears her murmur.

She opens the first cage and enters. The dog with the throat-wound is somehow still breathing. She bends over it, speaks to it. Faintly it wags its tail.

'Lucy!' he calls again, and now for the first time she turns her gaze on him. A frown appears on her face. 'What on earth did they do to you?' she says.

'My dearest child!' he says. He follows her into the cage and tries to take her in his arms. Gently, decisively, she wriggles loose.

The living-room is in a mess, so is his own room. Things have been taken: his jacket, his good shoes, and that is only the beginning of it.

He looks at himself in a mirror. Brown ash, all that is left of his hair, coats his scalp and forehead. Underneath it the scalp is an angry pink. He touches the skin: it is painful and beginning to ooze. One eyelid is swelling shut; his eyebrows are gone, his eyelashes too.

97

He goes to the bathroom, but the door is closed. 'Don't come in,' says Lucy's voice.

'Are you all right? Are you hurt?'

Stupid questions; she does not reply.

He tries to wash off the ash under the kitchen tap, pouring glass after glass of water over his head. Water trickles down his back; he begins to shiver with cold.

It happens every day, every hour, every minute, he tells himself, in every quarter of the country. Count yourself lucky to have escaped with your life. Count yourself lucky not to be a prisoner in the car at this moment, speeding away, or at the bottom of a donga with a bullet in your head. Count Lucy lucky too. Above all Lucy.

A risk to own anything: a car, a pair of shoes, a packet of cigarettes. Not enough to go around, not enough cars, shoes, cigarettes. Too many people, too few things. What there is must go into circulation, so that everyone can have a chance to be happy for a day. That is the theory; hold to the theory and to the comfort of theory. Not human evil, just a vast circulatory system, to whose workings pity and terror are irrelevant. That is how one must see life in this country: in its schematic aspect. Otherwise one could go mad. Cars, shoes; women too. There must be some niche in the system for women and what happens to them.

Lucy has come up behind him. She is wearing slacks and raincoat now; her hair is combed back, her face clean and entirely blank. He looks into her eyes. 'My dearest, dearest . . .' he says, and chokes on a sudden surge of tears.

She does not stir a finger to soothe him. 'Your head looks terrible,' she remarks. 'There's baby-oil in the bathroom cabinet. Put some on. Is your car gone?'

'Yes. I think they went off in the Port Elizabeth direction. I must telephone the police.'

'You can't. The telephone is smashed.'

She leaves him. He sits on the bed and waits. Though he has wrapped a blanket around himself, he continues to shiver. One of his wrists is swollen and throbbing with pain. He cannot recollect how he hurt it. It is already getting dark. The whole afternoon seems to have passed in a flash.

Lucy returns. 'They've let down the tyres of the kombi,' she says. 'I'm walking over to Ettinger's. I won't be long.' She pauses. 'David, when people ask, would you mind keeping to your own story, to what happened to you?'

He does not understand.

'You tell what happened to you, I tell what happened to me,' she repeats.

'You're making a mistake,' he says in a voice that is fast descending to a croak.

'No I'm not,' she says.

'My child, my child!' he says, holding out his arms to her. When she does not come, he puts aside his blanket, stands up, and takes her in his arms. In his embrace she is stiff as a pole, yielding nothing.

TWELVE

ETTINGER IS A SURLY old man who speaks English with a marked German accent. His wife is dead, his children have gone back to Germany, he is the only one left in Africa. He arrives in his three-litre pickup with Lucy at his side and waits with the engine running.

'Yes, I never go anywhere without my Beretta,' he observe once they are on the Grahamstown road. He pats the holster at his hip. 'The best is, you save yourself, because the police are not going to save you, not any more, you can be sure.'

Is Ettinger right? If he had had a gun, would he have saved Lucy? He doubts it. If he had had a gun, he would probably be dead now, he and Lucy both.

His hands, he notices, are trembling ever so lightly. Lucy has her arms folded across her breasts. Is that because she is trembling too?

He was expecting Ettinger to take them to the police station. But, it turns out, Lucy has told him to drive to the hospital.

'For my sake or for yours?' he asks her.

'For yours.'

'Won't the police want to see me too?'

'There is nothing you can tell them that I can't,' she replies. 'O is there?'

At the hospital she strides ahead through the door marke

CASUALTIES, fills out the form for him, seats him in the waiting room. She is all strength, all purposefulness, whereas the trembling seems to have spread to his whole body.

'If they discharge you, wait here,' she instructs him. 'I will be back to fetch you.'

'What about yourself?'

She shrugs. If she is trembling, she shows no sign of it.

He finds a seat between two hefty girls who might be sisters, one of them holding a moaning child, and a man with bloody wadding over his hand. He is twelfth in line. The clock on the wall says 5.45. He closes his good eye and slips into a swoon in which the two sisters continue to whisper together, *chuchotantes*. When he opens his eye the clock still says 5.45. Is it broken? No: the minute hand jerks and comes to rest on 5.46.

Two hours pass before a nurse calls him, and there is more waiting before his turn comes to see the sole doctor on duty, a young Indian woman.

The burns on his scalp are not serious, she says, though he must be wary of infection. She spends more time on his eye. The upper and lower lids are stuck together; separating them proves extraordinarily painful.

'You are lucky,' she comments after the examination. 'There is no damage to the eye itself. If they had used petrol it would be a different story.'

He emerges with his head dressed and bandaged, his eye covered, an ice-pack strapped to his wrist. In the waiting-room he is surprised to find Bill Shaw. Bill, who is a head shorter than he, grips him by the shoulders. 'Shocking, absolutely shocking,' he says. 'Lucy is over at our place. She was going to fetch you herself but Bev wouldn't hear of it. How are you?'

'I'm all right. Light burns, nothing serious. I'm sorry we've ruined your evening.'

'Nonsense!' says Bill Shaw. 'What else are friends for? You would have done the same.'

Spoken without irony, the words stay with him and will not go away. Bill Shaw believes that if he, Bill Shaw, had been hit over the head and set on fire, then he, David Lurie, would have driven to the hospital and sat waiting, without so much as a newspaper to read, to fetch him home. Bill Shaw believes that, because he and David Lurie once had a cup of tea together, David Lurie is his friend, and the two of them have obligations towards each other. Is Bill Shaw wrong or right? Has Bill Shaw, who was born in Hankey, not two hundred kilometres away, and works in a hardware shop, seen so little of the world that he does not know there are men who do not readily make friends, whose attitude toward friendships between men is corroded with scepticism? Modern English *friend* from Old English *freond*, from *freon*, to love. Does the drinking of tea seal a love-bond, in the eyes of Bill Shaw? Yet but for Bill and Bev Shaw, but for old Ettinger, but for bonds of some kind, where would he be now? On the ruined farm with the broken telephone amid the dead dogs.

'A shocking business,' says Bill Shaw again in the car. 'Atrocious. It's bad enough when you read about it in the paper, but when it happens to someone you know' – he shakes his head – 'that really brings it home to you. It's like being in a war all over again.'

He does not bother to reply. The day is not dead yet but living. *War, atrocity*: every word with which one tries to wrap up this day, the day swallows down its black throat.

Bev Shaw meets them at the door. Lucy has taken a sedative, she announces, and is lying down; best not to disturb her.

'Has she been to the police?'

'Yes, there's a bulletin out for your car.'

'And she has seen a doctor?'

'All attended to. How about you? Lucy says you were badly burned.'

'I have burns, but they are not as bad as they look.'

'Then you should eat and get some rest.'

'I'm not hungry.'

She runs water for him in their big, old-fashioned, cast-iron bath. He stretches out his pale length in the steaming water and tries to relax. But when it is time to get out, he slips and almost falls: he is as weak as a baby, and lightheaded too. He has to call Bill Shaw and suffer the ignominy of being helped out of the bath, helped to dry himself, helped into borrowed pyjamas. Later he hears Bill and Bev talking in low voices, and knows it is he they are talking about.

He has come away from the hospital with a tube of painkillers, a packet of burn dressings, and a little aluminium gadget to prop his head on. Bev Shaw settles him on a sofa that smells of cats; with surprising ease he falls asleep. In the middle of the night he awakes in a state of the utmost clarity. He has had a vision: Lucy has spoken to him; her words – 'Come to me, save me!' – still echo in his ears. In the vision she stands, hands outstretched, wet hair combed back, in a field of white light.

He gets up, stumbles against a chair, sends it flying. A light goes on and Bev Shaw is before him in her nightdress. 'I have to speak to Lucy,' he mumbles: his mouth is dry, his tongue thick.

The door to Lucy's room opens. Lucy is not at all as in the vision. Her face is puffy with sleep, she is tying the belt of a dressing-gown that is clearly not hers.

'I'm sorry, I had a dream,' he says. The word *vision* is suddenly too old-fashioned, too queer. 'I thought you were calling me.'

Lucy shakes her head. 'I wasn't. Go to sleep now.'

She is right, of course. It is three in the morning. But he cannot fail to notice that for the second time in a day she has spoken to him as if to a child – a child or an old man.

He tries to get back to sleep but cannot. It must be an effect of the pills, he tells himself: not a vision, not even a dream, just a chemical hallucination. Nevertheless, the figure of the woman in the field of light stays before him. 'Save me!' cries his daughter, her words clear, ringing, immediate. Is it possible that Lucy's soul did indeed leave her body and come to him? May people who do not believe in souls yet have them, and may their souls lead an independent life?

Hours yet before sunrise. His wrist aches, his eyes burn, his scalp is sore and irritable. Cautiously he switches on the lamp and gets up. With a blanket wrapped around him he pushes open Lucy's door and enters. There is a chair by the bedside; he sits down. His senses tell him she is awake.

What is he doing? He is watching over his little girl, guarding her from harm, warding off the bad spirits. After a long while he feels her begin to relax. A soft pop as her lips separate, and the gentlest of snores.

It is morning. Bev Shaw serves him a breakfast of cornflakes and tea, then disappears into Lucy's room.

'How is she?' he asks when she comes back.

Bev Shaw responds only with a terse shake of the head. Not your business, she seems to be saying. Menstruation, childbirth, violation and its aftermath: blood-matters; a woman's burden, women's preserve.

Not for the first time, he wonders whether women would not be happier living in communities of women, accepting visits from men only when they choose. Perhaps he is wrong to think of Lucy as homosexual. Perhaps she simply prefers female company. Or perhaps that is all that lesbians are: women who have no need of men.

No wonder they are so vehement against rape, she and Helen. Rape, god of chaos and mixture, violator of seclusions. Raping a lesbian worse than raping a virgin: more of a blow. Did they know what they were up to, those men? Had the word got around?

At nine o'clock, after Bill Shaw has gone off to work, he taps on Lucy's door. She is lying with her face turned to the wall. He sits down beside her, touches her cheek. It is wet with tears.

'This is not an easy thing to talk about,' he says, 'but have you seen a doctor?'

She sits up and blows her nose. 'I saw my GP last night.'

'And is he taking care of all eventualities?'

'She,' she says. 'She, not he. No' – and now there is a crack of anger in her voice – 'how can she? How can a doctor take care of all eventualities? Have some sense!'

He gets up. If she chooses to be irritable, then he can be irritable too. 'I'm sorry I asked,' he says. 'What are our plans for today?'

'Our plans? To go back to the farm and clean up.'

'And then?'

'Then to go on as before.'

'On the farm?'

'Of course. On the farm.'

'Be sensible, Lucy. Things have changed. We can't just pick up where we left off.'

'Why not?'

'Because it's not a good idea. Because it's not safe.'

'It was never safe, and it's not an idea, good or bad. I'm not going back for the sake of an idea. I'm just going back.'

Sitting up in her borrowed nightdress, she confronts him, neck stiff, eyes glittering. Not her father's little girl, not any longer.

THIRTEEN

BEFORE THEY SET off he needs to have his dressings changed. In the cramped little bathroom Bev Shaw unwinds the bandages. The eyelid is still closed and blisters have risen on his scalp, but the damage is not as bad as it could have been. The most painful part is the flange of his right ear: it is, as the young doctor put it, the only part of him that actually caught fire.

With a sterile solution Bev washes the exposed pink underskin of the scalp, then, using tweezers, lays the oily yellow dressing over it. Delicately she anoints the folds of his eyelid and his ear. She does not speak while she works. He recalls the goat in the clinic, wonders whether, submitting to her hands, it felt the same peacefulness.

'There,' she says at last, standing back.

He inspects the image in the mirror, with its neat white cap and blanked-out eye. 'Shipshape,' he remarks, but thinks: Like a mummy.

He tries again to raise the subject of the rape. 'Lucy says she saw her GP last night.'

'Yes.'

'There's the risk of pregnancy,' he presses on. 'There's the risk of venereal infection. There's the risk of HIV. Shouldn't she see a gynaecologist as well?'

Bev Shaw shifts uncomfortably. 'You must ask Lucy yourself.'

'I have asked. I can't get sense from her.'

'Ask again.'

It is past eleven, but Lucy shows no sign of emerging. Aimlessly he roams about the garden. A grey mood is settling on him. It is not just that he does not know what to do with himself. The events of yesterday have shocked him to the depths. The trembling, the weakness are only the first and most superficial signs of that shock. He has a sense that, inside him, a vital organ has been bruised, abused – perhaps even his heart. For the first time he has a taste of what it will be like to be an old man, tired to the bone, without hopes, without desires, indifferent to the future. Slumped on a plastic chair amid the stench of chicken feathers and rotting apples, he feels his interest in the world draining from him drop by drop. It may take weeks, it may take months before he is bled dry, but he is bleeding. When that is finished, he will be like a fly-casing in a spiderweb, brittle to the touch, lighter than rice-chaff, ready to float away.

He cannot expect help from Lucy. Patiently, silently, Lucy must work her own way back from the darkness to the light. Until she is herself again, the onus is on him to manage their daily life. But it has come too suddenly. It is a burden he is not ready for: the farm, the garden, the kennels. Lucy's future, his future, the future of the land as a whole – it is all a matter of indifference, he wants to say; let it all go to the dogs, I do not care. As for the men who visited them, he wishes them harm, wherever they may be, but otherwise does not want to think about them.

Just an after-effect, he tells himself, an after-effect of the invasion. In a while the organism will repair itself, and I, the ghost within it, will be my old self again. But the truth, he knows, is otherwise. His pleasure in living has been snuffed out. Like a leaf on a stream, like a puffball on a breeze, he has begun to float toward his end. He sees it quite clearly, and it fills him with (the word will not go away) despair. The blood of life is leaving his body and despair is taking its place, despair that is like a gas, odourless, tasteless, without nourishment. You breathe it in, your limbs relax, you cease to care, even at the moment when the steel touches your throat.

There is a ring at the doorbell: two young policemen in spruce new uniforms, ready to begin their investigations. Lucy emerges from her room looking haggard, wearing the same clothes as yesterday. She refuses breakfast. With the police following behind in their van, Bev drives them out to the farm.

The corpses of the dogs lie in the cage where they fell. The bulldog Katy is still around: they catch a glimpse of her skulking near the stable, keeping her distance. Of Petrus there is no sign.

Indoors, the two policemen take off their caps, tuck them under their arms. He stands back, leaves it to Lucy to take them through the story she has elected to tell. They listen respectfully, taking down her every word, the pen darting nervously across the pages of the notebook. They are of her generation, but edgy of her nevertheless, as if she were a creature polluted and her pollution could leap across to them, soil them.

There were three men, she recites, or two men and a boy. They tricked their way into the house, took (she lists the items) money, clothes, a television set, a CD player, a rifle with ammunition. When her father resisted, they assaulted him, poured spirits over him, tried to set him on fire. Then they shot the dogs and drove off in his car. She describes the men and what they were wearing; she describes the car.

All the while she speaks, Lucy looks steadily at him, as though drawing strength from him, or else daring him to contradict her. When one of the officers asks, 'How long did the whole incident take?' she says, 'Twenty minutes, thirty minutes.' An untruth, as he knows, as she knows. It took much longer. How much longer?

As much longer as the men needed to finish off their business with the lady of the house.

Nevertheless he does not interrupt. *A matter of indifference*: he barely listens as Lucy goes through her story. Words are beginning to take shape that have been hovering since last night at the edges of memory. *Two old ladies locked in the lavatory / They were there from Monday to Saturday / Nobody knew they were there*. Locked in the lavatory while his daughter was used. A chant from his childhood come back to point a jeering finger. *Oh dear, what can the matter be?* Lucy's secret; his disgrace.

Cautiously the policemen move through the house, inspecting. No blood, no overturned furniture. The mess in the kitchen has been cleaned up (by Lucy? when?). Behind the lavatory door, two spent matchsticks, which they do not even notice.

In Lucy's room the double bed is stripped bare. *The scene of the crime,* he thinks to himself; and, as if reading the thought, the policemen avert their eyes, pass on.

A quiet house on a winter morning, no more, no less.

'A detective will come and take fingerprints,' they say as they leave. 'Try not to touch things. If you remember anything else they took, give us a call at the station.'

Barely have they departed when the telephone repairmen arrive, then old Ettinger. Of the absent Petrus, Ettinger remarks darkly, 'Not one of them you can trust.' He will send a boy, he says, to fix the kombi.

In the past he has seen Lucy fly into a rage at the use of the word *boy*. Now she does not react.

He walks Ettinger to the door.

'Poor Lucy,' remarks Ettinger. 'It must have been bad for her. Still, it could have been worse.'

'Indeed? How?'

'They could have taken her away with them.'

That brings him up short. No fool, Ettinger.

At last he and Lucy are alone. 'I will bury the dogs if you show me where,' he offers. 'What are you going to tell the owners?'

'I'll tell them the truth.'

'Will your insurance cover it?'

'I don't know. I don't know whether insurance policies cover massacres. I will have to find out.'

A pause. 'Why aren't you telling the whole story, Lucy?'

'I have told the whole story. The whole story is what I have told.'

He shakes his head dubiously. 'I am sure you have your reasons, but in a wider context are you sure this is the best course?'

She does not reply, and he does not press her, for the moment. But his thoughts go to the three intruders, the three invaders, men he will probably never lay eyes on again, yet forever part of his life now, and of his daughter's. The men will watch the newspapers, listen to the gossip. They will read that they are being sought for robbery and assault and nothing else. It will dawn on them that over the body of the woman silence is being drawn like a blanket. *Too ashamed*, they will say to each other, *too ashamed to tell*, and they will chuckle luxuriously, recollecting their exploit. Is Lucy prepared to concede them that victory?

He digs the hole where Lucy tells him, close to the boundary line. A grave for six full-grown dogs: even in the recently ploughed earth it takes him the best part of an hour, and by the time he has finished his back is sore, his arms are sore, his wrist aches again. He trundles the corpses over in a wheelbarrow. The dog with the hole in its throat still bares its bloody teeth. Like shooting fish in a barrel, he thinks. Contemptible, yet exhilarating, probably, in a country where dogs are bred to snarl at the mere smell of a black man. A satisfying afternoon's work, heady, like all revenge. One by one he tumbles the dogs into the hole, then fills it in.

He returns to find Lucy installing a camp-bed in the musty little pantry that she uses for storage.

'For whom is this?' he asks.

'For myself.'

'What about the spare room?'

'The ceiling-boards have gone.'

'And the big room at the back?'

'The freezer makes too much noise.'

Not true. The freezer in the back room barely purrs. It is because of what the freezer holds that Lucy will not sleep there: offal, bones, butcher's meat for dogs that no longer have need of it.

'Take over my room,' he says. 'I'll sleep here.' And at once he sets about clearing out his things.

But does he really want to move into this cell, with its boxes of empty preserve-jars piled in a corner and its single tiny south-facing window? If the ghosts of Lucy's violators still hover in her bedroom, then surely they ought to be chased out, not allowed to take it over as their sanctum. So he moves his belongings into Lucy's room.

Evening falls. They are not hungry, but they eat. Eating is a ritual, and rituals make things easier.

As gently as he can, he offers his question again. 'Lucy, my dearest, why don't you want to tell? It was a crime. There is no shame in being the object of a crime. You did not choose to be the object. You are an innocent party.'

Sitting across the table from him, Lucy draws a deep breath, gathers herself, then breathes out again and shakes her head.

'Can I guess?' he says. 'Are you trying to remind me of something?'

'Am I trying to remind you of what?'

'Of what women undergo at the hands of men.'

'Nothing could be further from my thoughts. This has nothing to do with you, David. You want to know why I have not laid a particular charge with the police. I will tell you, as long as you agree not to raise the subject again. The reason is that, as far as I am concerned, what happened to me is a purely private matter. In another time, in another place it might be held to be a public matter. But in this place, at this time, it is not. It is my business, mine alone.'

'This place being what?'

'This place being South Africa.'

'I don't agree. I don't agree with what you are doing. Do you think that by meekly accepting what happened to you, you can set yourself apart from farmers like Ettinger? Do you think what happened here was an exam: if you come through, you get a diploma and safe conduct into the future, or a sign to paint on the door-lintel that will make the plague pass you by? That is not how vengeance works, Lucy. Vengeance is like a fire. The more it devours, the hungrier it gets.'

'Stop it, David! I don't want to hear this talk of plagues and fires. I am not just trying to save my skin. If that is what you think, you miss the point entirely.'

'Then help me. Is it some form of private salvation you are trying to work out? Do you hope you can expiate the crimes of the past by suffering in the present?'

'No. You keep misreading me. Guilt and salvation are abstractions. I don't act in terms of abstractions. Until you make an effort to see that, I can't help you.'

He wants to respond, but she cuts him short. 'David, we agreed. I don't want to go on with this conversation.'

Never yet have they been so far and so bitterly apart. He is shaken.

FOURTEEN

A NEW DAY. Ettinger telephones, offering to lend them a gun 'for the meanwhile'. 'Thank you,' he replies. 'We'll think about it.'

He gets out Lucy's tools and repairs the kitchen door as well as he is able. They ought to install bars, security gates, a perimeter fence, as Ettinger has done. They ought to turn the farmhouse into a fortress. Lucy ought to buy a pistol and a two-way radio, and take shooting lessons. But will she ever consent? She is here because she loves the land and the old, *ländliche* way of life. If that way of life is doomed, what is left for her to love?

Katy is coaxed out of her hiding-place and settled in the kitchen. She is subdued and timorous, following Lucy about, keeping close to her heels. Life, from moment to moment, is not as before. The house feels alien, violated; they are continually on the alert, listening for sounds.

Then Petrus makes his return. An old lorry groans up the rutted driveway and stops beside the stable. Petrus steps down from the cab, wearing a suit too tight for him, followed by his wife and the driver. From the back of the lorry the two men unload cartons, creosoted poles, sheets of galvanized iron, a roll of plastic piping, and finally, with much noise and commotion, two halfgrown sheep, which Petrus tethers to a fence-post. The lorry makes a wide sweep around the stable and thunders back down the driveway. Petrus and his wife disappear inside. A plume of smoke begins to rise from the asbestos-pipe chimney.

He continues to watch. In a while, Petrus's wife emerges and with a broad, easy movement empties a slop bucket. A handsome woman, he thinks to himself, with her long skirt and her headcloth piled high, country fashion. A handsome woman and a lucky man. But where have they been?

'Petrus is back,' he tells Lucy. 'With a load of building materials.'

'Good.'

'Why didn't he tell you he was going away? Doesn't it strike you as fishy that he should disappear at precisely this time?'

'I can't order Petrus about. He is his own master.'

A non sequitur, but he lets it pass. He has decided to let everything pass, with Lucy, for the time being.

Lucy keeps to herself, expresses no feelings, shows no interest in anything around her. It is he, ignorant as he is about farming, who must let the ducks out of their pen, master the sluice system and lead water to save the garden from parching. Lucy spends hour after hour lying on her bed, staring into space or looking at old magazines, of which she seems to have an unlimited store. She flicks through them impatiently, as though searching for something that is not there. Of *Edwin Drood* there is no more sign.

He spies Petrus out at the dam, in his work overalls. It seems odd that the man has not yet reported to Lucy. He strolls over, exchanges greetings. 'You must have heard, we had a big robbery on Wednesday while you were away.'

'Yes,' says Petrus, 'I heard. It is very bad, a very bad thing. But you are all right now.'

Is he all right? Is Lucy all right? Is Petrus asking a question? It does not sound like a question, but he cannot take it otherwise, not decently. The question is, what is the answer?

'I am alive,' he says. 'As long as one is alive one is all right, I suppose. So yes, I am all right.' He pauses, waits, allows a silence to develop, a silence which Petrus ought to fill with the next question: *And how is Lucy?*

He is wrong. 'Will Lucy go to the market tomorrow?' asks Petrus.

'I don't know.'

'Because she will lose her stall if she does not go,' says Petrus.

'Maybe.'

'Petrus wants to know if you are going to market tomorrow,' he informs Lucy. 'He is afraid you might lose your stall.'

'Why don't the two of you go,' she says. 'I don't feel up to it.'

'Are you sure? It would be a pity to miss a week.'

She does not reply. She would rather hide her face, and he knows why. Because of the disgrace. Because of the shame. That is what their visitors have achieved; that is what they have done to this confident, modern young woman. Like a stain the story is spreading across the district. Not her story to spread but theirs: they are its owners. How they put her in her place, how they showed her what a woman was for.

With his one eye and his white skullcap, he has his own measure of shyness about showing himself in public. But for Lucy's sake he goes through with the market business, sitting beside Petrus at the stall, enduring the stares of the curious, responding politely to those friends of Lucy's who choose to commiserate. 'Yes, we lost a car,' he says. 'And the dogs, of course, all but one. No, my daughter is fine, just not feeling well today. No, we are not hopeful, the police are overstretched, as I'm sure you know. Yes, I'll be sure to tell her.'

He reads their story as reported in the *Herald*. *Unknown assailants* the men are called. 'Three unknown assailants have attacked Ms Lucy Lourie and her elderly father on their smallholding outside

Salem, making off with clothes, electronic goods and a firearm. In a bizarre twist, the robbers also shot and killed six watchdogs before escaping in a 1993 Toyota Corolla, registration CA 507644. Mr Lourie, who received light injuries during the attack, was treated at Settlers Hospital and discharged.'

He is glad that no connection is made between Ms Lourie's elderly father and David Lurie, disciple of nature poet William Wordsworth and until recently professor at the Cape Technical University.

As for the actual trading, there is little for him to do. Petrus is the one who swiftly and efficiently lays out their wares, the one who knows the prices, takes the money, makes the change. Petrus is in fact the one who does the work, while he sits and warms his hands. Just like the old days: *baas en Klaas*. Except that he does not presume to give Petrus orders. Petrus does what needs to be done, and that is that.

Nevertheless, their takings are down: less than three hundred rand. The reason is Lucy's absence, no doubt about that. Boxes of flowers, bags of vegetables have to be loaded back into the kombi. Petrus shakes his head. 'Not good,' he says.

As yet Petrus has offered no explanation for his absence. Petrus has the right to come and go as he wishes; he has exercised that right; he is entitled to his silence. But questions remain. Does Petrus know who the strangers were? Was it because of some word Petrus let drop that they made Lucy their target rather than, say, Ettinger? Did Petrus know in advance what they were planning?

In the old days one could have had it out with Petrus. In the old days one could have had it out to the extent of losing one's temper and sending him packing and hiring someone in his place. But though Petrus is paid a wage, Petrus is no longer, strictly speaking, hired help. It is hard to say what Petrus is, strictly speaking. The word that seems to serve best, however, is *neighbour*. Petrus is a neighbour who at present happens to sell his labour, because that is what suits him. He sells his labour under contract, unwritten contract, and that contract makes no provision for dismissal on grounds of suspicion. It is a new world they live in, he and Lucy and Petrus. Petrus knows it, and he knows it, and Petrus knows that he knows it.

In spite of which he feels at home with Petrus, is even prepared, however guardedly, to like him. Petrus is a man of his generation. Doubtless Petrus has been through a lot, doubtless he has a story to tell. He would not mind hearing Petrus's story one day. But preferably not reduced to English. More and more he is convinced that English is an unfit medium for the truth of South Africa. Stretches of English code whole sentences long have thickened, lost their articulations, their articulateness, their articulatedness. Like a dinosaur expiring and settling in the mud, the language has stiffened. Pressed into the mould of English, Petrus's story would come out arthritic, bygone.

What appeals to him in Petrus is his face, his face and his hands. If there is such a thing as honest toil, then Petrus bears its marks. A man of patience, energy, resilience. A peasant, a *paysan*, a man of the country. A plotter and a schemer and no doubt a liar too, like peasants everywhere. Honest toil and honest cunning.

He has his own suspicions of what Petrus is up to, in the longer run. Petrus will not be content to plough forever his hectare and a half. Lucy may have lasted longer than her hippie, gypsy friends, but to Petrus Lucy is still chickenfeed: an amateur, an enthusiast of the farming life rather than a farmer. Petrus would like to take over Lucy's land. Then he would like to have Ettinger's too, or enough of it to run a herd on. Ettinger will be a harder nut to crack. Lucy is merely a transient; Ettinger is another peasant, a man of the earth, tenacious, *eingewurzelt*. But Ettinger will die one of these days, and the Ettinger son has fled. In that respect Ettinger has been stupid. A good peasant takes care to have lots of sons.

Petrus has a vision of the future in which people like Lucy have no place. But that need not make an enemy of Petrus. Country life has always been a matter of neighbours scheming against each other, wishing on each other pests, poor crops, financial ruin, yet in a crisis ready to lend a hand.

The worst, the darkest reading would be that Petrus engaged three strange men to teach Lucy a lesson, paying them off with the loot. But he cannot believe that, it would be too simple. The real truth, he suspects, is something far more – he casts around for the word – *anthropological*, something it would take months to get to the bottom of, months of patient, unhurried conversation with dozens of people, and the offices of an interpreter.

On the other hand, he does believe that Petrus knew something was in the offing; he does believe Petrus could have warned Lucy. That is why he will not let go of the subject. That is why he continues to nag Petrus.

Petrus has emptied the concrete storage dam and is cleaning it of algae. It is an unpleasant job. Nevertheless, he offers to help. With his feet crammed into Lucy's rubber boots, he climbs into the dam, stepping carefully on the slick bottom. For a while he and Petrus work in concert, scraping, scrubbing, shovelling out the mud. Then he breaks off.

'Do you know, Petrus,' he says, 'I find it hard to believe the men who came here were strangers. I find it hard to believe they arrived out of nowhere, and did what they did, and disappeared afterwards like ghosts. And I find it hard to believe that the reason they picked on us was simply that we were the first white folk they met that day. What do you think? Am I wrong?'

Petrus smokes a pipe, an old-fashioned pipe with a hooked stem and a little silver cap over the bowl. Now he straightens up, takes the pipe from the pocket of his overalls, opens the cap, tamps down the tobacco in the bowl, sucks at the pipe unlit. He stares reflectively over the dam wall, over the hills, over open country. His expression is perfectly tranquil.

'The police must find them,' he says at last. 'The police must find them and put them in jail. That is the job of the police.'

'But the police are not going to find them without help. Those men knew about the forestry station. I am convinced they knew about Lucy. How could they have known if they were complete strangers to the district?'

Petrus chooses not to take this as a question. He puts the pipe away in his pocket, exchanges spade for broom.

'It was not simply theft, Petrus,' he persists. 'They did not come just to steal. They did not come just to do this to me.' He touches the bandages, touches the eye-shield. 'They came to do something else as well. You know what I mean, or if you don't know you can surely guess. After they did what they did, you cannot expect Lucy calmly to go on with her life as before. I am Lucy's father. I want those men to be caught and brought before the law and punished. Am I wrong? Am I wrong to want justice?'

He does not care how he gets the words out of Petrus now, he just wants to hear them.

'No, you are not wrong.'

A flurry of anger runs through him, strong enough to take him by surprise. He picks up his spade and strikes whole strips of mud and weed from the dam-bottom, flinging them over his shoulder, over the wall. *You are whipping yourself into a rage*, he admonishes himself: *Stop it!* Yet at this moment he would like to take Petrus by the throat. *If it had been your wife instead of my daughter*, he would like to say to Petrus, *you would not be tapping your pipe and weighing your words so judiciously*. *Violation*: that is the word he would like to force out of Petrus. *Yes, it was a violation*, he would like to hear Petrus say; *yes, it was an outrage*.

In silence, side by side, he and Petrus finish off the job.

This is how his days are spent on the farm. He helps Petrus clean up the irrigation system. He keeps the garden from going to ruin. He packs produce for the market. He helps Bev Shaw at the clinic. He sweeps the floors, cooks the meals, does all the things that Lucy no longer does. He is busy from dawn to dusk.

His eye is healing surprisingly fast: after a mere week he is able to use it again. The burns are taking longer. He retains the skullcap and the bandage over his ear. The ear, uncovered, looks like a naked pink mollusc: he does not know when he will be bold enough to expose it to the gaze of others.

He buys a hat to keep off the sun, and, to a degree, to hide his face. He is trying to get used to looking odd, worse than odd, repulsive – one of those sorry creatures whom children gawk at in the street. 'Why does that man look so funny?' they ask their mothers, and have to be hushed.

He goes to the shops in Salem as seldom as he can, to Grahamstown only on Saturdays. All at once he has become a recluse, a country recluse. The end of roving. Though the heart be still as loving and the moon be still as bright. Who would have thought it would come to an end so soon and so suddenly: the roving, the loving!

He has no reason to believe their misfortunes have made it on to the gossip circuit in Cape Town. Nevertheless, he wants to be sure that Rosalind does not hear the story in some garbled form. Twice he tries to call her, without success. The third time he telephones the travel agency where she works. Rosalind is in Madagascar, he is told, scouting; he is given the fax number of a hotel in Antananarivo.

He composes a dispatch: 'Lucy and I have had some bad luck. My car was stolen, and there was a scuffle too, in which I took a bit of a knock. Nothing serious – we're both fine, though shaken. Thought I'd let you know in case of rumours. Trust you are having a good time.' He gives the page to Lucy to approve, then to Bev Shaw to send off. To Rosalind in darkest Africa.

Lucy is not improving. She stays up all night, claiming she cannot sleep; then in the afternoons he finds her asleep on the sofa, her thumb in her mouth like a child. She has lost interest in food: he is the one who has to tempt her to eat, cooking unfamiliar dishes because she refuses to touch meat.

This is not what he came for – to be stuck in the back of beyond, warding off demons, nursing his daughter, attending to a dying enterprise. If he came for anything, it was to gather himself, gather his forces. Here he is losing himself day by day.

The demons do not pass him by. He has nightmares of his own in which he wallows in a bed of blood, or, panting, shouting soundlessly, runs from the man with the face like a hawk, like a Benin mask, like Thoth. One night, half sleepwalking, half demented, he strips his own bed, even turns the mattress over, looking for stains.

There is still the Byron project. Of the books he brought from Cape Town, only two volumes of the letters are left – the rest were in the trunk of the stolen car. The public library in Grahamstown can offer nothing but selections from the poems. But does he need to go on reading? What more does he need to know of how Byron and his acquaintance passed their time in old Ravenna? Can he not, by now, invent a Byron who is true to Byron, and a Teresa too?

He has, if the truth be told, been putting it off for months: the moment when he must face the blank page, strike the first note, see what he is worth. Snatches are already imprinted on his mind of the lovers in duet, the vocal lines, soprano and tenor, coiling wordlessly around and past each other like serpents. Melody without climax; the whisper of reptile scales on marble staircases; and, throbbing in the background, the baritone of the humiliated husband. Will this be where the dark trio are at last brought to life: not in Cape Town but in old Kaffraria?

FIFTEEN

THE TWO YOUNG sheep are tethered all day beside the stable on a bare patch of ground. Their bleating, steady and monotonous, has begun to annoy him. He strolls over to Petrus, who has his bicycle upside down and is working on it. 'Those sheep,' he says – 'don't you think we could tie them where they can graze?'

'They are for the party,' says Petrus. 'On Saturday I will slaughter them for the party. You and Lucy must come.' He wipes his hands clean. 'I invite you and Lucy to the party.'

'On Saturday?'

'Yes, I am giving a party on Saturday. A big party.'

'Thank you. But even if the sheep are for the party, don't you think they could graze?'

An hour later the sheep are still tethered, still bleating dolefully. Petrus is nowhere to be seen. Exasperated, he unties them and tugs them over to the damside, where there is abundant grass.

The sheep drink at length, then leisurely begin to graze. They are black-faced Persians, alike in size, in markings, even in their movements. Twins, in all likelihood, destined since birth for the butcher's knife. Well, nothing remarkable in that. When did a sheep last die of old age? Sheep do not own themselves, do not own their lives. They exist to be used, every last ounce of them, their flesh to be eaten, their bones to be crushed and fed to poultry.

Nothing escapes, except perhaps the gall bladder, which no one will eat. Descartes should have thought of that. The soul, suspended in the dark, bitter gall, hiding.

'Petrus has invited us to a party,' he tells Lucy. 'Why is he throwing a party?'

'Because of the land transfer, I would guess. It goes through officially on the first of next month. It's a big day for him. We should at least put in an appearance, take them a present.'

'He is going to slaughter the two sheep. I wouldn't have thought two sheep would go very far.'

'Petrus is a pennypincher. In the old days it would have been an ox.'

'I'm not sure I like the way he does things – bringing the slaughter-beasts home to acquaint them with the people who are going to eat them.'

'What would you prefer? That the slaughtering be done in an abattoir, so that you needn't think about it?'

'Yes.'

'Wake up, David. This is the country. This is Africa.'

There is a snappishness to Lucy nowadays that he sees no justification for. His usual response is to withdraw into silence. There are spells when the two of them are like strangers in the same house.

He tells himself that he must be patient, that Lucy is still living in the shadow of the attack, that time needs to pass before she will be herself. But what if he is wrong? What if, after an attack like that, one is never oneself again? What if an attack like that turns one into a different and darker person altogether?

There is an even more sinister explanation for Lucy's moodiness, one that he cannot put from his mind. 'Lucy,' he asks the same day, out of the blue, 'you aren't hiding something from me, are you? You didn't pick up something from those men?'

She is sitting on the sofa in pyjamas and dressing-gown, playing with the cat. It is past noon. The cat is young, alert, skittish. Lucy dangles the belt of the gown before it. The cat slaps at the belt, quick, light paw-blows, one-two-three-four.

'Men?' she says. 'Which men?' She flicks the belt to one side; the cat dives after it.

Which men? His heart stops. Has she gone mad? Is she refusing to remember?

But, it would appear, she is only teasing him. 'David, I am not a child any more. I have seen a doctor, I have had tests, I have done everything one can reasonably do. Now I can only wait.'

'I see. And by *wait* you mean wait for what I think you mean?'

'Yes.'

'How long will that take?'

She shrugs. 'A month. Three months. Longer. Science has not yet put a limit on how long one has to wait. For ever, maybe.'

The cat makes a quick pounce at the belt, but the game is over now.

He sits down beside his daughter; the cat jumps off the sofa, stalks away. He takes her hand. Now that he is close to her, a faint smell of staleness, unwashedness, reaches him. 'At least it won't be for ever, my dearest,' he says. 'At least you will be spared that.'

The sheep spend the rest of the day near the dam where he has tethered them. The next morning they are back on the barren patch beside the stable.

Presumably they have until Saturday morning, two days. It seems a miserable way to spend the last two days of one's life. Country ways – that is what Lucy calls this kind of thing. He has other words: indifference, hardheartedness. If the country can pass judgment on the city, then the city can pass judgment on the country too.

He has thought of buying the sheep from Petrus. But what will that accomplish? Petrus will only use the money to buy new slaughter-animals, and pocket the difference. And what will he do with the sheep anyway, once he has bought them out of slavery? Set them free on the public road? Pen them up in the dog-cages and feed them hay?

A bond seems to have come into existence between himself and the two Persians, he does not know how. The bond is not one of affection. It is not even a bond with these two in particular, whom he could not pick out from a mob in a field. Nevertheless, suddenly and without reason, their lot has become important to him.

He stands before them, under the sun, waiting for the buzz in his mind to settle, waiting for a sign.

There is a fly trying to creep into the ear of one of them. The ear twitches. The fly takes off, circles, returns, settles. The ear twitches again.

He takes a step forward. The sheep backs away uneasily to the limit of its chain.

He remembers Bev Shaw nuzzling the old billy-goat with the ravaged testicles, stroking him, comforting him, entering into his life. How does she get it right, this communion with animals? Some trick he does not have. One has to be a certain kind of person, perhaps, with fewer complications.

The sun beats on his face in all its springtime radiance. Do I have to change, he thinks? Do I have to become like Bev Shaw?

He speaks to Lucy. 'I have been thinking about this party of Petrus's. On the whole, I would prefer not to go. Is that possible without being rude?'

'Anything to do with his slaughter-sheep?'

'Yes. No. I haven't changed my ideas, if that is what you mean. I still don't believe that animals have properly individual lives.

Which among them get to live, which get to die, is not, as far as I am concerned, worth agonizing over. Nevertheless . . .'

'Nevertheless?'

'Nevertheless, in this case I am disturbed. I can't say why.'

'Well, Petrus and his guests are certainly not going to give up their mutton chops out of deference to you and your sensibilities.'

'I'm not asking for that. I would just prefer not to be one of the party, not this time. I'm sorry. I never imagined I would end up talking this way.'

'God moves in mysterious ways, David.'

'Don't mock me.'

Saturday is looming, market day. 'Should we run the stall?' he asks Lucy. She shrugs. 'You decide,' she says. He does not run the stall. He does not query her decision; in fact he is relieved.

Preparations for Petrus's festivities begin at noon on Saturday with the arrival of a band of women half a dozen strong, wearing what looks to him like churchgoing finery. Behind the stable they get a fire going. Soon there comes on the wind the stench of boiling offal, from which he infers that the deed has been done, the double deed, that it is all over.

Should he mourn? Is it proper to mourn the death of beings who do not practise mourning among themselves? Looking into his heart, he can find only a vague sadness.

Too close, he thinks: we live too close to Petrus. It is like sharing a house with strangers, sharing noises, sharing smells.

He knocks at Lucy's door. 'Do you want to go for a walk?' he asks.

'Thanks, but no. Take Katy.'

He takes the bulldog, but she is so slow and sulky that he grows irritated, chases her back to the farm, and sets off alone on an eight-kilometre loop, walking fast, trying to tire himself out.

At five o'clock the guests start arriving, by car, by taxi, on foot. He watches from behind the kitchen curtain. Most are of their host's generation, staid, solid. There is one old woman over whom a particular fuss is made: wearing his blue suit and a garish pink shirt, Petrus comes all the way down the path to welcome her.

It is dark before the younger folk make an appearance. On the breeze comes a murmur of talk, laughter and music, music that he associates with the Johannesburg of his own youth. Quite tolerable, he thinks to himself – quite jolly, even.

'It's time,' says Lucy. 'Are you coming?'

Unusually, she is wearing a knee-length dress and high heels, with a necklace of painted wooden beads and matching earrings. He is not sure he likes the effect.

'All right, I'll come. I'm ready.'

'Haven't you got a suit here?'

'No.'

'Then at least put on a tie.'

'I thought we were in the country.'

'All the more reason to dress up. This is a big day in Petrus's life.'

She carries a tiny flashlight. They walk up the track to Petrus's house, father and daughter arm in arm, she lighting the way, he bearing their offering.

At the open door they pause, smiling. Petrus is nowhere to be seen, but a little girl in a party dress comes up and leads them in.

The old stable has no ceiling and no proper floor, but at least it is spacious and at least it has electricity. Shaded lamps and pictures on the walls (Van Gogh's sunflowers, a Tretchikoff lady in blue, Jane Fonda in her Barbarella outfit, Doctor Khumalo scoring a goal) soften the bleakness.

They are the only whites. There is dancing going on, to the old-fashioned African jazz he had heard. Curious glances are cast at the two of them, or perhaps only at his skullcap.

128

Lucy knows some of the women. She commences introductions. Then Petrus appears at their side. He does not play the eager host, does not offer them a drink, but does say, 'No more dogs. I am not any more the dog-man,' which Lucy chooses to accept as a joke; so all, it appears, is well.

'We have brought you something,' says Lucy; 'but perhaps we should give it to your wife. It is for the house.'

From the kitchen area, if that is what they are to call it, Petrus summons his wife. It is the first time he has seen her from close by. She is young – younger than Lucy – pleasant-faced rather than pretty, shy, clearly pregnant. She takes Lucy's hand but does not take his, nor does she meet his eyes.

Lucy speaks a few words in Xhosa and presents her with the package. There are by now half a dozen onlookers around them.

'She must unwrap it,' says Petrus.

'Yes, you must unwrap it,' says Lucy.

Carefully, at pains not to tear the festive paper with its mandolins and sprigs of laurel, the young wife opens the package. It is a cloth in a rather attractive Ashanti design. 'Thank you,' she whispers in English.

'It's a bedspread,' Lucy explains to Petrus.

'Lucy is our benefactor,' says Petrus; and then, to Lucy: 'You are our benefactor.'

A distasteful word, it seems to him, double-edged, souring the moment. Yet can Petrus be blamed? The language he draws on with such aplomb is, if he only knew it, tired, friable, eaten from the inside as if by termites. Only the monosyllables can still be relied on, and not even all of them.

What is to be done? Nothing that he, the one-time teacher of communications, can see. Nothing short of starting all over again with the ABC. By the time the big words come back reconstructed, purified, fit to be trusted once more, he will be long dead.

He shivers, as if a goose has trodden on his grave.

'The baby – when are you expecting the baby?' he asks Petrus's wife.

She looks at him uncomprehendingly.

'In October,' Petrus intervenes. 'The baby is coming in October. We hope he will be a boy.'

'Oh. What have you got against girls?'

'We are praying for a boy,' says Petrus. 'Always it is best if the first one is a boy. Then he can show his sisters – show them how to behave. Yes.' He pauses. 'A girl is very expensive.' He rubs thumb and forefinger together. 'Always money, money, money.'

A long time since he last saw that gesture. Used of Jews, in the old days: money-money-money, with the same meaningful cock of the head. But presumably Petrus is innocent of that snippet of European tradition.

'Boys can be expensive too,' he remarks, doing his bit for the conversation.

'You must buy them this, you must buy them that,' continues Petrus, getting into his stride, no longer listening. 'Now, today, the man does not pay for the woman. *I* pay.' He floats a hand above his wife's head; modestly she drops her eyes. '*I* pay. But that is old fashion. Clothes, nice things, it is all the same: pay, pay, pay.' He repeats the finger-rubbing. 'No, a boy is better. Except your daughter. Your daughter is different. Your daughter is as good as a boy. Almost!' He laughs at his sally. 'Hey, Lucy!'

Lucy smiles, but he knows she is embarrassed. 'I'm going to dance,' she murmurs, and moves away.

On the floor she dances by herself in the solipsistic way that now seems to be the mode. Soon she is joined by a young man, tall, loose-limbed, nattily dressed. He dances opposite her, snapping his fingers, flashing her smiles, courting her.

Women are beginning to come in from outside, carrying trays

of grilled meat. The air is full of appetizing smells. A new contingent of guests floods in, young, noisy, lively, not old fashion at all. The party is getting into its swing.

A plate of food finds its way into his hands. He passes it on to Petrus. 'No,' says Petrus – 'is for you. Otherwise we are passing plates all night.'

Petrus and his wife are spending a lot of time with him, making him feel at home. Kind people, he thinks. Country people.

He glances across at Lucy. The young man is dancing only inches from her now, lifting his legs high and thumping them down, pumping his arms, enjoying himself.

The plate he is holding contains two mutton chops, a baked potato, a ladle of rice swimming in gravy, a slice of pumpkin. He finds a chair to perch on, sharing it with a skinny old man with rheumy eyes. I am going to eat this, he says to himself. I am going to eat it and ask forgiveness afterwards.

Then Lucy is at his side, breathing fast, her face tense. 'Can we leave?' she says. 'They are here.'

'Who is here?'

'I saw one of them out at the back. David, I don't want to kick up a fuss, but can we leave at once?'

'Hold this.' He passes her the plate, goes out at the back door.

There are almost as many guests outside as inside, clustered around the fire, talking, drinking, laughing. From the far side of the fire someone is staring at him. At once things fall into place. He knows that face, knows it intimately. He thrusts his way past the bodies. *I am going to be kicking up a fuss*, he thinks. *A pity, on this of all days. But some things will not wait.*

In front of the boy he plants himself. It is the third of them, the dull-faced apprentice, the running-dog. 'I know you,' he says grimly.

The boy does not appear to be startled. On the contrary, the boy appears to have been waiting for this moment, storing himself up for it. The voice that issues from his throat is thick with rage. 'Who are you?' he says, but the words mean something else: *By what right are you here?* His whole body radiates violence.

Then Petrus is with them, talking fast in Xhosa.

He lays a hand on Petrus's sleeve. Petrus breaks off, gives him an impatient glare. 'Do you know who this is?' he asks Petrus.

'No, I do not know what this is,' says Petrus angrily. 'I do not know what is the trouble. What is the trouble?'

'He – this thug – was here before, with his pals. He is one of them. But let *him* tell you what it is about. Let *him* tell you why he is wanted by the police.'

'It is not true!' shouts the boy. Again he speaks to Petrus, a stream of angry words. Music continues to unfurl into the night air, but no one is dancing any longer: Petrus's guests are clustering around them, pushing, jostling, interjecting. The atmosphere is not good.

Petrus speaks. 'He says he does not know what you are talking about.'

'He is lying. He knows perfectly well. Lucy will confirm.'

But of course Lucy will not confirm. How can he expect Lucy to come out before these strangers, face the boy, point a finger, say, *Yes, he is one of them. He was one of those who did the deed*?

'I am going to telephone the police,' he says.

There is a disapproving murmur from the onlookers.

'I am going to telephone the police,' he repeats to Petrus. Petrus is stony-faced.

In a cloud of silence he returns indoors, where Lucy stands waiting. 'Let's go,' he says.

The guests give way before them. No longer is there friendliness in their aspect. Lucy has forgotten the flashlight: they lose their way in the dark; Lucy has to take off her shoes; they blunder through potato beds before they reach the farmhouse.

He has the telephone in his hand when Lucy stops him. 'David, no, don't do it. It's not Petrus's fault. If you call in the police, the evening will be destroyed for him. Be sensible.'

He is astonished, astonished enough to turn on his daughter. 'For God's sake, why isn't it Petrus's fault? One way or another, it was he who brought in those men in the first place. And now he has the effrontery to invite them back. Why should I be sensible? Really, Lucy, from beginning to end I fail to understand. I fail to understand why you did not lay *real* charges against them, and now I fail to understand why you are protecting Petrus. Petrus is not an innocent party, Petrus is *with* them.'

'Don't shout at me, David. This is my life. I am the one who has to live here. What happened to me is my business, mine alone, not yours, and if there is one right I have it is the right not to be put on trial like this, not to have to justify myself – not to you, not to anyone else. As for Petrus, he is not some hired labourer whom I can sack because in my opinion he is mixed up with the wrong people. That's all gone, gone with the wind. If you want to antagonize Petrus, you had better be sure of your facts first. You can't call in the police. I won't have it. Wait until morning. Wait until you have heard Petrus's side of the story.'

'But in the meantime the boy will disappear!'

'He won't disappear. Petrus knows him. In any event, no one disappears in the Eastern Cape. It's not that kind of place.'

'Lucy, Lucy, I plead with you! You want to make up for the wrongs of the past, but this is not the way to do it. If you fail to stand up for yourself at this moment, you will never be able to hold your head up again. You may as well pack your bags and leave. As for the police, if you are too delicate to call them in now, then we should never have involved them in the first place. We should just have kept quiet and waited for the next attack. Or cut our own throats.'

'Stop it, David! I don't need to defend myself before you. *You don't know what happened.*'

'I don't know?'

'No, you don't begin to know. Pause and think about that. With regard to the police, let me remind you why we called them in in the first place: for the sake of the insurance. We filed a report because if we did not, the insurance would not pay out.'

'Lucy, you amaze me. That is simply not true, and you know it. As for Petrus, I repeat: if you buckle at this point, if you fail, you will not be able to live with yourself. You have a duty to yourself, to the future, to your own self-respect. Let me call the police. Or call them yourself.'

'No.'

No: that is Lucy's last word to him. She retires to her room, closes the door on him, closes him out. Step by step, as inexorably as if they were man and wife, he and she are being driven apart, and there is nothing he can do about it. Their very quarrels have become like the bickerings of a married couple, trapped together with nowhere else to go. How she must be rueing the day when he came to live with her! She must wish him gone, and the sooner the better.

Yet she too will have to leave, in the long run. As a woman alone on a farm she has no future, that is clear. Even the days of Ettinger, with his guns and barbed wire and alarm systems, are numbered. If Lucy has any sense she will quit before a fate befalls her worse than a fate worse than death. But of course she will not. She is stubborn, and immersed, too, in the life she has chosen.

He slips out of the house. Treading cautiously in the dark, he approaches the stable from behind.

The big fire has died down, the music has stopped. There is a cluster of people at the back door, a door built wide enough to admit a tractor. He peers over their heads.

In the centre of the floor stands one of the guests, a man of middle age. He has a shaven head and a bull neck; he wears a dark suit and, around his neck, a gold chain from which hangs a medal the size of a fist, of the kind that chieftains used to have bestowed on them as a symbol of office. Symbols struck by the boxful in a foundry in Coventry or Birmingham; stamped on the one side with the head of sour Victoria, *regina et imperatrix*, on the other with gnus or ibises rampant. Medals, Chieftains, for the use of. Shipped all over the old Empire: to Nagpur, Fiji, the Gold Coast, Kaffraria.

The man is speaking, orating in rounded periods that rise and fall. He has no idea what the man is saying, but every now and then there is a pause and a murmur of agreement from his audience, among whom, young and old, a mood of quiet satisfaction seems to reign.

He looks around. The boy is standing nearby, just inside the door. The boy's eyes flit nervously across him. Other eyes turn toward him too: toward the stranger, the odd one out. The man with the medal frowns, falters for a moment, raises his voice.

As for him, he does not mind the attention. Let them know I am still here, he thinks, let them know I am not skulking in the big house. And if that spoils their get-together, so be it. He lifts a hand to his white skullcap. For the first time he is glad to have it, to wear it as his own.

SIXTEEN

ALL OF THE next morning Lucy avoids him. The meeting she promised with Petrus does not take place. Then in the afternoon Petrus himself raps at the back door, businesslike as ever, wearing boots and overalls. It is time to lay the pipes, he says. He wants to lay PVC piping from the storage dam to the site of his new house, a distance of two hundred metres. Can he borrow tools, and can David help him fit the regulator?

'I know nothing about regulators. I know nothing about plumbing.' He is in no mood to be helpful to Petrus.

'It is not plumbing,' says Petrus. 'It is pipefitting. It is just laying pipes.'

On the way to the dam Petrus talks about regulators of different kinds, about pressure-valves, about junctions; he brings out the words with a flourish, showing off his mastery. The new pipe will have to cross Lucy's land, he says; it is good that she has given her permission. She is 'forward-looking'. 'She is a forward-looking lady, not backward-looking.'

About the party, about the boy with the flickering eyes, Petrus says nothing. It is as though none of that had happened.

His own role at the dam soon becomes clear. Petrus needs him not for advice on pipefitting or plumbing but to hold things, to pass him tools — to be his *handlanger*, in fact. The role is not one he objects to. Petrus is a good workman, it is an education to watch him. It is Petrus himself he has begun to dislike. As Petrus drones on about his plans, he grows more and more frosty toward him. He would not wish to be marooned with Petrus on a desert isle. He would certainly not wish to be married to him. A dominating personality. The young wife seems happy, but he wonders what stories the old wife has to tell.

At last, when he has had enough, he cuts across the flow. 'Petrus,' he says, 'that young man who was at your house last night – what is his name and where is he now?'

Petrus takes off his cap, wipes his forehead. Today he is wearing a peaked cap with a silver South African Railways and Harbours badge. He seems to have a collection of headgear.

'You see,' says Petrus, frowning, 'David, it is a hard thing you are saying, that this boy is a thief. He is very angry that you are calling him a thief. That is what he is telling everyone. And I, I am the one who must be keeping the peace. So it is hard for me too.'

'I have no intention of involving you in the case, Petrus. Tell me the boy's name and whereabouts and I will pass on the information to the police. Then we can leave it to the police to investigate and bring him and his friends to justice. You will not be involved, I will not be involved, it will be a matter for the law.'

Petrus stretches, bathing his face in the sun's glow. 'But the insurance will give you a new car.'

Is it a question? A declaration? What game is Petrus playing? 'The insurance will not give me a new car,' he explains, trying to be patient. 'Assuming it isn't bankrupt by now because of all the car-theft in this country, the insurance will give me a percentage of its own idea of what the old car was worth. That won't be enough to buy a new car. Anyhow, there is a principle involved. We can't leave it to insurance companies to deliver justice. That is not their business.'

'But you will not get your car back from this boy. He cannot give you your car. He does not know where your car is. Your car is gone. The best is, you buy another car with the insurance, then you have a car again.'

How has he landed in this dead-end? He tries a new tack. 'Petrus, let me ask you, is this boy related to you?'

'And why', Petrus continues, ignoring the question, 'do you want to take this boy to the police? He is too young, you cannot put him in jail.'

'If he is eighteen he can be tried. If he is sixteen he can be tried.'

'No, no, he is not eighteen.'

'How do you know? He looks eighteen to me, he looks more than eighteen.'

'I know, I know! He is just a youth, he cannot go to jail, that is the law, you cannot put a youth in jail, you must let him go!'

For Petrus that seems to clinch the argument. Heavily he settles on one knee and begins to work the coupling over the outlet pipe.

'Petrus, my daughter wants to be a good neighbour – a good citizen and a good neighbour. She loves the Eastern Cape. She wants to make her life here, she wants to get along with everyone. But how can she do so when she is liable to be attacked at any moment by thugs who then escape scot-free? Surely you see!'

Petrus is struggling to get the coupling to fit. The skin of his hands shows deep, rough cracks; he gives little grunts as he works; there is no sign he has even heard.

'Lucy is safe here,' he announces suddenly. 'It is all right. You can leave her, she is safe.'

'But she is not safe, Petrus! Clearly she is not safe! You know what happened here on the twenty-first.'

'Yes, I know what happened. But now it is all right.'

'Who says it is all right?'

'I say.'

'You say? You will protect her?'

'I will protect her.'

'You didn't protect her last time.'

Petrus smears more grease over the pipe.

'You say you know what happened, but you didn't protect her last time,' he repeats. 'You went away, and then those three thugs turned up, and now it seems you are friends with one of them. What am I supposed to conclude?'

It is the closest he has come to accusing Petrus. But why not?

'The boy is not guilty,' says Petrus. 'He is not a criminal. He is not a thief.'

'It is not just thieving I am speaking of. There was another crime as well, a far heavier crime. You say you know what happened. You must know what I mean.'

'He is not guilty. He is too young. It is just a big mistake.'

'You know?'

'I know.' The pipe is in. Petrus folds the clamp, tightens it, stands up, straightens his back. 'I know. I am telling you. I know.'

'You know. You know the future. What can I say to that? You have spoken. Do you need me here any longer?'

'No, now it is easy, now I must just dig the pipe in.'

Despite Petrus's confidence in the insurance industry, there is no movement on his claim. Without a car he feels trapped on the farm.

On one of his afternoons at the clinic, he unburdens himself to Bev Shaw. 'Lucy and I are not getting on,' he says. 'Nothing remarkable in that, I suppose. Parents and children aren't made to live together. Under normal circumstances I would have moved out by now, gone back to Cape Town. But I can't leave Lucy alone on the farm. She isn't safe. I am trying to persuade her to hand over the operation to Petrus and take a break. But she won't listen to me.'

'You have to let go of your children, David. You can't watch over Lucy for ever.'

'I let go of Lucy long ago. I have been the least protective of fathers. But the present situation is different. Lucy is objectively in danger. We have had that demonstrated to us.'

'It will be all right. Petrus will take her under his wing.'

'Petrus? What interest has Petrus in taking her under his wing?'

'You underestimate Petrus. Petrus slaved to get the market garden going for Lucy. Without Petrus Lucy wouldn't be where she is now. I am not saying she owes him everything, but she owes him a lot.'

'That may be so. The question is, what does Petrus owe her?'

'Petrus is a good old chap. You can depend on him.'

'Depend on Petrus? Because Petrus has a beard and smokes a pipe and carries a stick, you think Petrus is an old-style kaffir. But it is not like that at all. Petrus is not an old-style kaffir, much less a good old chap. Petrus, in my opinion, is itching for Lucy to pull out. If you want proof, look no further than at what happened to Lucy and me. It may not have been Petrus's brainchild, but he certainly turned a blind eye, he certainly didn't warn us, he certainly took care not to be in the vicinity.'

His vehemence surprises Bev Shaw. 'Poor Lucy,' she whispers: 'she has been through such a lot!'

'I know what Lucy has been through. I was there.'

Wide-eyed she gazes back at him. 'But you weren't there, David. She told me. You weren't.'

You weren't there. You don't know what happened. He is baffled. Where, according to Bev Shaw, according to Lucy, was he not? In the room where the intruders were committing their outrages? Do they think he does not know what rape is? Do they think he has not suffered with his daughter? What more could he have witnessed than he is capable of imagining? Or do they think that, where rape is concerned, no man can be where the woman is? Whatever the answer, he is outraged, outraged at being treated like an outsider.

He buys a small television set to replace the one that was stolen. In the evenings, after supper, he and Lucy sit side by side on the sofa watching the news and then, if they can bear it, the entertainment.

It is true, the visit has gone on too long, in his opinion as well as in Lucy's. He is tired of living out of a suitcase, tired of listening all the while for the crunch of gravel on the pathway. He wants to be able to sit at his own desk again, sleep in his own bed. But Cape Town is far away, almost another country. Despite Bev's counsel, despite Petrus's assurances, despite Lucy's obstinacy, he is not prepared to abandon his daughter. This is where he lives, for the present: in this time, in this place.

He has recovered the sight of his eye completely. His scalp is healing over; he need no longer use the oily dressing. Only the ear still needs daily attention. So time does indeed heal all. Presumably Lucy is healing too, or if not healing then forgetting, growing scar tissue around the memory of that day, sheathing it, sealing it off. So that one day she may be able to say, 'The day we were robbed,' and think of it merely as the day when they were robbed.

He tries to spend the daytime hours outdoors, leaving Lucy free to breathe in the house. He works in the garden; when he is tired he sits by the dam, observing the ups and downs of the duck family, brooding on the Byron project.

The project is not moving. All he can grasp of it are fragments. The first words of the first act still resist him; the first notes remain as elusive as wisps of smoke. Sometimes he fears that the characters in the story, who for more than a year have been his ghostly companions, are beginning to fade away. Even the most appealing of them, Margarita Cogni, whose passionate contralto attacks hurled against Byron's bitch-mate Teresa Guiccioli he aches to hear, is slipping. Their loss fills him with despair, despair as grey and even and unimportant, in the larger scheme, as a headache.

He goes off to the Animal Welfare clinic as often as he can, offering himself for whatever jobs call for no skill: feeding, cleaning, mopping up.

The animals they care for at the clinic are mainly dogs, less frequently cats: for livestock, D Village appears to have its own veterinary lore, its own pharmacopoeia, its own healers. The dogs that are brought in suffer from distempers, from broken limbs, from infected bites, from mange, from neglect, benign or malign, from old age, from malnutrition, from intestinal parasites, but most of all from their own fertility. There are simply too many of them. When people bring a dog in they do not say straight out, 'I have brought you this dog to kill,' but that is what is expected: that they will dispose of it, make it disappear, dispatch it to oblivion. What is being asked for is, in fact, *Lösung* (German always to hand with an appropriately blank abstraction): sublimation, as alcohol is sublimed from water, leaving no residue, no aftertaste.

So on Sunday afternoons the clinic door is closed and locked while he helps Bev Shaw *lösen* the week's superfluous canines. One at a time he fetches them out of the cage at the back and leads or carries them into the theatre. To each, in what will be its last minutes, Bev gives her fullest attention, stroking it, talking to it, easing its passage. If, more often than not, the dog fails to be charmed, it is because of his presence: he gives off the wrong smell (*They can smell your thoughts*), the smell of shame. Nevertheless, he is the one who holds the dog still as the needle finds the vein and the drug hits the heart and the legs buckle and the eyes dim.

He had thought he would get used to it. But that is not what happens. The more killings he assists in, the more jittery he gets. One Sunday evening, driving home in Lucy's kombi, he actually has to stop at the roadside to recover himself. Tears flow down his face that he cannot stop; his hands shake.

He does not understand what is happening to him. Until now he has been more or less indifferent to animals. Although in an abstract way he disapproves of cruelty, he cannot tell whether by nature he is cruel or kind. He is simply nothing. He assumes that people from whom cruelty is demanded in the line of duty, people who work in slaughterhouses, for instance, grow carapaces over their souls. Habit hardens: it must be so in most cases, but it does not seem to be so in his. He does not seem to have the gift of hardness.

His whole being is gripped by what happens in the theatre. He is convinced the dogs know their time has come. Despite the silence and the painlessness of the procedure, despite the good thoughts that Bev Shaw thinks and that he tries to think, despite the airtight bags in which they tie the newmade corpses, the dogs in the yard smell what is going on inside. They flatten their ears, they droop their tails, as if they too feel the disgrace of dying; locking their legs, they have to be pulled or pushed or carried over the threshold. On the table some snap wildly left and right, some whine plaintively; none will look straight at the needle in Bev's hand, which they somehow know is going to harm them terribly.

Worst are those that sniff him and try to lick his hand. He has never liked being licked, and his first impulse is to pull away. Why pretend to be a chum when in fact one is a murderer? But then he relents. Why should a creature with the shadow of death upon it feel him flinch away as if its touch were abhorrent? So he lets them lick him, if they want to, just as Bev Shaw strokes them and kisses them if they will let her.

He is not, he hopes, a sentimentalist. He tries not to sentimentalize the animals he kills, or to sentimentalize Bev Shaw. He avoids saying to her, 'I don't know how you do it,' in order not to have to hear her say in return, 'Someone has to do it.' He does not dismiss the possibility that at the deepest level Bev Shaw may be not a liberating angel but a devil, that beneath her show of compassion may hide a heart as leathery as a butcher's. He tries to keep an open mind.

Since Bev Shaw is the one who inflicts the needle, it is he who takes charge of disposing of the remains. The morning after each killing session he drives the loaded kombi to the grounds of Settlers Hospital, to the incinerator, and there consigns the bodies in their black bags to the flames.

It would be simpler to cart the bags to the incinerator immediately after the session and leave them there for the incinerator crew to dispose of. But that would mean leaving them on the dump with the rest of the weekend's scourings: with waste from the hospital wards, carrion scooped up at the roadside, malodorous refuse from the tannery – a mixture both casual and terrible. He is not prepared to inflict such dishonour upon them.

So on Sunday evenings he brings the bags to the farm in the back of Lucy's kombi, parks them overnight, and on Monday mornings drives them to the hospital grounds. There he himself loads them, one at a time, on to the feeder trolley, cranks the mechanism that hauls the trolley through the steel gate into the flames, pulls the lever to empty it of its contents, and cranks it back, while the workmen whose job this normally is stand by and watch.

On his first Monday he left it to them to do the incinerating. Rigor mortis had stiffened the corpses overnight. The dead legs caught in the bars of the trolley, and when the trolley came back from its trip to the furnace, the dog would as often as not come riding back too, blackened and grinning, smelling of singed fur, its plastic covering burnt away. After a while the workmen began to beat the bags with the backs of their shovels before loading them, to break the rigid limbs. It was then that he intervened and took over the job himself.

The incinerator is anthracite-fuelled, with an electric fan to suck air through the flues; he guesses that it dates from the 1950s, when the hospital itself was built. It operates six days of the week, Monday to Saturday. On the seventh day it rests. When the crew arrive for work they first rake out the ashes from the previous day, then charge the fire. By nine a.m. temperatures of a thousand degrees centigrade are being generated in the inner chamber, hot enough to calcify bone. The fire is stoked until mid-morning; it takes all afternoon to cool down.

He does not know the names of the crew and they do not know his. To them he is simply the man who began arriving on Mondays with the bags from Animal Welfare and has since then been turning up earlier and earlier. He comes, he does his work, he goes; he does not form part of the society of which the incinerator, despite the wire fence and the padlocked gate and the notice in three languages, is the hub.

For the fence has long ago been cut through; the gate and the notice are simply ignored. By the time the orderlies arrive in the morning with the first bags of hospital waste, there are already numbers of women and children waiting to pick through it for syringes, pins, washable bandages, anything for which there is a market, but particularly for pills, which they sell to *muti* shops or trade in the streets. There are vagrants too, who hang about the hospital grounds by day and sleep by night against the wall of the incinerator, or perhaps even in the tunnel, for the warmth.

It is not a sodality he tries to join. But when he is there, they are there; and if what he brings to the dump does not interest them, that is only because the parts of a dead dog can neither be sold nor be eaten.

Why has he taken on this job? To lighten the burden on Bev

Shaw? For that it would be enough to drop off the bags at the dump and drive away. For the sake of the dogs? But the dogs are dead; and what do dogs know of honour and dishonour anyway?

For himself, then. For his idea of the world, a world in which men do not use shovels to beat corpses into a more convenient shape for processing.

The dogs are brought to the clinic because they are unwanted: *because we are too menny*. That is where he enters their lives. He may not be their saviour, the one for whom they are not too many, but he is prepared to take care of them once they are unable, utterly unable, to take care of themselves, once even Bev Shaw has washed her hands of them. A dog-man, Petrus once called himself. Well, now he has become a dog-man: a dog undertaker; a dog psychopomp; a *harijan*.

Curious that a man as selfish as he should be offering himself to the service of dead dogs. There must be other, more productive ways of giving oneself to the world, or to an idea of the world. One could for instance work longer hours at the clinic. One could try to persuade the children at the dump not to fill their bodies with poisons. Even sitting down more purposefully with the Byron libretto might, at a pinch, be construed as a service to mankind.

But there are other people to do these things – the animal welfare thing, the social rehabilitation thing, even the Byron thing. He saves the honour of corpses because there is no one else stupid enough to do it. That is what he is becoming: stupid, daft, wrongheaded.

SEVENTEEN

THEIR WORK AT the clinic is over for the Sunday. The kombi is loaded with its dead freight. As a last chore he is mopping the floor of the surgery.

'I'll do that,' says Bev Shaw, coming in from the yard. 'You'll be wanting to get back.'

'I'm in no hurry.'

'Still, you must be used to a different kind of life.'

'A different kind of life? I didn't know life came in kinds.'

'I mean, you must find life very dull here. You must miss your own circle. You must miss having women friends.'

'Women friends, you say. Surely Lucy told you why I left Cape Town. Women friends didn't bring me much luck there.'

'You shouldn't be hard on her.'

'Hard on Lucy? I don't have it in me to be hard on Lucy.'

'Not Lucy – the young woman in Cape Town. Lucy says there was a young woman who caused you a lot of trouble.'

'Yes, there was a young woman. But I was the troublemaker in that case. I caused the young woman in question at least as much trouble as she caused me.'

'Lucy says you have had to give up your position at the university. That must have been difficult. Do you regret it?'

What nosiness! Curious how the whiff of scandal excites

women. Does this plain little creature think him incapable of shocking her? Or is being shocked another of the duties she takes on – like a nun who lies down to be violated so that the quota of violation in the world will be reduced?

'Do I regret it? I don't know. What happened in Cape Town brought me here. I'm not unhappy here.'

'But at the time – did you regret it at the time?'

'At the time? Do you mean, in the heat of the act? Of course not. In the heat of the act there are no doubts. As I'm sure you must know yourself.'

She blushes. A long time since he last saw a woman of middle age blush so thoroughly. To the roots of her hair.

'Still, you must find Grahamstown very quiet,' she murmurs. 'By comparison.'

'I don't mind Grahamstown. At least I am out of the way of temptation. Besides, I don't live in Grahamstown. I live on a farm with my daughter.'

Out of the way of temptation: a callous thing to say to a woman, even a plain one. Yet not plain in everyone's eyes. There must have been a time when Bill Shaw saw something in young Bev. Other men too, perhaps.

He tries to imagine her twenty years younger, when the upturned face on its short neck must have seemed pert and the freckled skin homely, healthy. On an impulse he reaches out and runs a finger over her lips.

She lowers her eyes but does not flinch. On the contrary, she responds, brushing her lips against his hand – even, it might be said, kissing it – while blushing furiously all the time.

That is all that happens. That is as far as they go. Without another word he leaves the clinic. Behind him he hears her switching off the lights.

The next afternoon there is a call from her. 'Can we meet at the clinic, at four,' she says. Not a question but an announcement, made in a high, strained voice. Almost he asks, 'Why?', but then has the good sense not to. Nonetheless he is surprised. He would bet she has not been down this road before. This must be how, in her innocence, she assumes adulteries are carried out: with the woman telephoning her pursuer, declaring herself ready.

The clinic is not open on Mondays. He lets himself in, turns the key behind him in the lock. Bev Shaw is in the surgery, standing with her back to him. He folds her in his arms; she nuzzles her ear against his chin; his lips brush the tight little curls of her hair. 'There are blankets,' she says. 'In the cabinet. On the bottom shelf.'

Two blankets, one pink, one grey, smuggled from her home by a woman who in the last hour has probably bathed and powdered and anointed herself in readiness; who has, for all he knows, been powdering and anointing herself every Sunday, and storing blankets in the cabinet, just in case. Who thinks, because he comes from the big city, because there is scandal attached to his name, that he makes love to many women and expects to be made love to by every woman who crosses his path.

The choice is between the operating table and the floor. He spreads out the blankets on the floor, the grey blanket underneath, the pink on top. He switches off the light, leaves the room, checks that the back door is locked, waits. He hears the rustle of clothes as she undresses. Bev. Never did he dream he would sleep with a Bev.

She is lying under the blanket with only her head sticking out. Even in the dimness there is nothing charming in the sight. Slipping off his underpants, he gets in beside her, runs his hands down her body. She has no breasts to speak of. Sturdy, almost waistless, like a squat little tub.

She grasps his hand, passes him something. A contraceptive. All

149

thought out beforehand, from beginning to end.

Of their congress he can at least say that he does his duty. Without passion but without distaste either. So that in the end Bev Shaw can feel pleased with herself. All she intended has been accomplished. He, David Lurie, has been succoured, as a man is succoured by a woman; her friend Lucy Lurie has been helped with a difficult visit.

Let me not forget this day, he tells himself, lying beside her when they are spent. After the sweet young flesh of Melanie Isaacs, this is what I have come to. This is what I will have to get used to, this and even less than this.

'It's late,' says Bev Shaw. 'I must be going.'

He pushes the blanket aside and gets up, making no effort to hide himself. Let her gaze her fill on her Romeo, he thinks, on his bowed shoulders and skinny shanks.

It is indeed late. On the horizon lies a last crimson glow; the moon looms overhead; smoke hangs in the air; across a strip of waste land, from the first rows of shacks, comes a hubbub of voices. At the door Bev presses herself against him a last time, rests her head on his chest. He lets her do it, as he has let her do everything she has felt a need to do. His thoughts go to Emma Bovary strutting before the mirror after her first big afternoon. *I have a lover! I have a lover!* sings Emma to herself. Well, let poor Bev Shaw go home and do some singing too. And let him stop calling her poor Bev Shaw. If she is poor, he is bankrupt.

EIGHTEEN

PETRUS HAS BORROWED a tractor, from where he has no idea, to which he has coupled the old rotary plough that has lain rusting behind the stable since before Lucy's time. In a matter of hours he has ploughed the whole of his land. All very swift and businesslike; all very unlike Africa. In olden times, that is to say ten years ago, it would have taken him days with a hand-plough and oxen.

Against this new Petrus what chance does Lucy stand? Petrus arrived as the dig-man, the carry-man, the water-man. Now he is too busy for that kind of thing. Where is Lucy going to find someone to dig, to carry, to water? Were this a chess game, he would say that Lucy has been outplayed on all fronts. If she had any sense she would quit: approach the Land Bank, work out a deal, consign the farm to Petrus, return to civilization. She could open boarding kennels in the suburbs; she could branch out into cats. She could even go back to what she and her friends did in their hippie days: ethnic weaving, ethnic pot-decoration, ethnic basket-weaving; selling beads to tourists.

Defeated. It is not hard to imagine Lucy in ten years' time: a heavy woman with lines of sadness on her face, wearing clothes long out of fashion, talking to her pets, eating alone. Not much of a life. But better than passing her days in fear of the next attack, when the dogs will not be enough to protect her and no one will answer the telephone.

He approaches Petrus on the site he has chosen for his new residence, on a slight rise overlooking the farmhouse. The surveyor has already paid his visit, the pegs are in place.

'You are not going to do the building yourself, are you?' he asks.

Petrus chuckles. 'No, it is a skill job, building,' he says. 'Bricklaying, plastering, all that, you need to be skill. No, I am going to dig the trenches. That I can do by myself. That is not such a skill job, that is just a job for a boy. For digging you just have to be a boy.'

Petrus speaks the word with real amusement. Once he was a boy, now he is no longer. Now he can play at being one, as Marie Antoinette could play at being a milkmaid.

He comes to the point. 'If Lucy and I went back to Cape Town, would you be prepared to keep her part of the farm running? We would pay you a salary, or you could do it on a percentage basis. A percentage of the profits.'

'I must keep Lucy's farm running,' says Petrus. 'I must be the *farm manager*.' He pronounces the words as if he has never heard them before, as if they have popped up before him like a rabbit out of a hat.

'Yes, we could call you the farm manager if you like.'

'And Lucy will come back one day.'

'I am sure she will come back. She is very attached to this farm. She has no intention of giving it up. But she has been having a hard time recently. She needs a break. A holiday.'

'By the sea,' says Petrus, and smiles, showing teeth yellow from smoking.

'Yes, by the sea, if she wants.' He is irritated by Petrus's habit of letting words hang in the air. There was a time when he thought he might become friends with Petrus. Now he detests him.

Talking to Petrus is like punching a bag filled with sand. 'I don't see that either of us is entitled to question Lucy if she decides to take a break,' he says. 'Neither you nor I.'

'How long I must be farm manager?'

'I don't know yet, Petrus. I haven't discussed it with Lucy, I am just exploring the possibility, seeing if you are agreeable.'

'And I must do all the things – I must feed the dogs, I must plant the vegetables, I must go to the market – '

'Petrus, there is no need to make a list. There won't be dogs. I am just asking in a general way, if Lucy took a holiday, would you be prepared to look after the farm?'

'How I must go to the market if I do not have the kombi?'

'That is a detail. We can discuss details later. I just want a general answer, yes or no.'

Petrus shakes his head. 'It is too much, too much,' he says.

Out of the blue comes a call from the police, from a Detective-Sergeant Esterhuyse in Port Elizabeth. His car has been recovered. It is in the yard at the New Brighton station, where he may identify and reclaim it. Two men have been arrested.

'That's wonderful,' he says. 'I had almost given up hope.'

'No, sir, the docket stays open two years.'

'What condition is the car in? Is it driveable?'

'Yes, you can drive it.'

In an unfamiliar state of elation he drives with Lucy to Port Elizabeth and then to New Brighton, where they follow directions to Van Deventer Street, to a flat, fortress-like police station surrounded by a two-metre fence topped with razor wire. Emphatic signs forbid parking in front of the station. They park far down the road.

'I'll wait in the car,' says Lucy.

'Are you sure?'

'I don't like this place. I'll wait.'

He presents himself at the charge office, is directed along a maze of corridors to the Vehicle Theft Unit. Detective-Sergeant Esterhuyse, a plump, blond little man, searches through his files, then conducts him to a yard where scores of vehicles stand parked bumper to bumper. Up and down the ranks they go.

'Where did you find it?' he asks Esterhuyse.

'Here in New Brighton. You were lucky. Usually with the older Corollas the buggers chop it up for parts.'

'You said you made arrests.'

'Two guys. We got them on a tipoff. Found a whole house full of stolen goods. TVs, videos, fridges, you name it.'

'Where are the men now?'

'They're out on bail.'

'Wouldn't it have made more sense to call me in before you set them free, to have me identify them? Now that they are out on bail they will just disappear. You know that.'

The detective is stiffly silent.

They stop before a white Corolla. 'This is not my car,' he says. 'My car had CA plates. It says so on the docket.' He points to the number on the sheet: CA 507644.

'They respray them. They put on false plates. They change plates around.'

'Even so, this is not my car. Can you open it?'

The detective opens the car. The interior smells of wet newspaper and fried chicken.

'I don't have a sound system,' he says. 'It's not my car. Are you sure my car isn't somewhere else in the lot?'

They complete their tour of the lot. His car is not there. Esterhuyse scratches his head. 'I'll check into it,' he says. 'There must be a mixup. Leave me your number and I'll give you a call.'

Lucy is sitting behind the wheel of the kombi, her eyes closed.

He raps on the window and she unlocks the door. 'It's all a mistake, he says, getting in. 'They have a Corolla, but it's not mine.'

'Did you see the men?'

'The men?'

'You said two men had been arrested.'

'They are out again on bail. Anyway, it's not my car, so whoever was arrested can't be whoever took my car.'

There is a long silence. 'Does that follow, logically?' she says.

She starts the engine, yanks fiercely on the wheel.

'I didn't realize you were keen for them to be caught,' he says. He can hear the irritation in his voice but does nothing to check it. 'If they are caught it means a trial and all that a trial entails. You will have to testify. Are you ready for that?'

Lucy switches off the engine. Her face is stiff as she fights off tears.

'In any event, the trail is cold. Our friends aren't going to be caught, not with the police in the state they are in. So let us forget about that.'

He gathers himself. He is becoming a nag, a bore, but there is no helping that. 'Lucy, it really is time for you to face up to your choices. Either you stay on in a house full of ugly memories and go on brooding on what happened to you, or you put the whole episode behind you and start a new chapter elsewhere. Those, as I see it, are the alternatives. I know you would like to stay, but shouldn't you at least consider the other route? Can't the two of us talk about it rationally?'

She shakes her head. 'I can't talk any more, David, I just can't,' she says, speaking softly, rapidly, as though afraid the words will dry up. 'I know I am not being clear. I wish I could explain. But I can't. Because of who you are and who I am, I can't. I'm sorry. And I'm sorry about your car. I'm sorry about the disappointment.'

She rests her head on her arms; her shoulders heave as she gives in.

Again the feeling washes over him: listlessness, indifference, but also weightlessness, as if he has been eaten away from inside and only the eroded shell of his heart remains. How, he thinks to himself, can a man in this state find words, find music that will bring back the dead?

Sitting on the sidewalk not five yards away, a woman in slippers and a ragged dress is staring fiercely at them. He lays a protective hand on Lucy's shoulder. *My daughter*, he thinks; *my dearest daughter. Whom it has fallen to me to guide. Who one of these days will have to guide me.*

Can she smell his thoughts?

It is he who takes over the driving. Halfway home, Lucy, to his surprise, speaks. 'It was so personal,' she says. 'It was done with such personal hatred. That was what stunned me more than anything. The rest was . . . expected. But why did they hate me so? I had never set eyes on them.'

He waits for more, but there is no more, for the moment. 'It was history speaking through them,' he offers at last. 'A history of wrong. Think of it that way, if it helps. It may have seemed personal, but it wasn't. It came down from the ancestors.'

'That doesn't make it easier. The shock simply doesn't go away. The shock of being hated, I mean. In the act.'

In the act. Does she mean what he thinks she means?

'Are you still afraid?' he asks.

'Yes.'

'Afraid they are going to come back?'

'Yes.'

'Did you think, if you didn't lay a charge against them with the police, they wouldn't come back? Was that what you told yourself?'

'No.'

'Then what?'

She is silent.

'Lucy, it could be so simple. Close down the kennels. Do it at once. Lock up the house, pay Petrus to guard it. Take a break for six months or a year, until things have improved in this country. Go overseas. Go to Holland. I'll pay. When you come back you can take stock, make a fresh start.'

'If I leave now, David, I won't come back. Thank you for the offer, but it won't work. There is nothing you can suggest that I haven't been through a hundred times myself.'

'Then what do you propose to do?'

'I don't know. But whatever I decide I want to decide by myself, without being pushed. There are things you just don't understand.'

'What don't I understand?'

'To begin with, you don't understand what happened to me that day. You are concerned for my sake, which I appreciate, you think you understand, but finally you don't. Because you can't.'

He slows down and pulls off the road. 'Don't,' says Lucy. 'Not here. This is a bad stretch, too risky to stop.'

He picks up speed. 'On the contrary, I understand all too well,' he says. 'I will pronounce the word we have avoided hitherto. You were raped. Multiply. By three men.'

'And?'

'You were in fear of your life. You were afraid that after you had been used you would be killed. Disposed of. Because you were nothing to them.'

'And?' Her voice is now a whisper.

'And I did nothing. I did not save you.'

That is his own confession.

She gives an impatient little flick of the hand. 'Don't blame yourself, David. You couldn't have been expected to rescue me. If they had come a week earlier, I would have been alone in the house. But you are right, I meant nothing to them, nothing. I could feel it.'

There is a pause. 'I think they have done it before,' she resumes, her voice steadier now. 'At least the two older ones have. I think they are rapists first and foremost. Stealing things is just incidental. A side-line. I think they *do* rape.'

'You think they will come back?'

'I think I am in their territory. They have marked me. They will come back for me.'

'Then you can't possibly stay.'

'Why not?'

'Because that would be an invitation to them to return.'

She broods a long while before she answers. 'But isn't there another way of looking at it, David? What if . . . what if *that* is the price one has to pay for staying on? Perhaps that is how they look at it; perhaps that is how I should look at it too. They see me as owing something. They see themselves as debt collectors, tax collectors. Why should I be allowed to live here without paying? Perhaps that is what they tell themselves.'

'I am sure they tell themselves many things. It is in their interest to make up stories that justify them. But trust your feelings. You said you felt only hatred from them.'

'Hatred . . . When it comes to men and sex, David, nothing surprises me any more. Maybe, for men, hating the woman makes sex more exciting. You are a man, you ought to know. When you have sex with someone strange – when you trap her, hold her down, get her under you, put all your weight on her – isn't it a bit like killing? Pushing the knife in; exiting afterwards, leaving the body behind covered in blood – doesn't it feel like murder, like getting away with murder?'

You are a man, you ought to know: does one speak to one's father like that? Are she and he on the same side?

'Perhaps,' he says. 'Sometimes. For some men.' And then rapidly, without forethought: 'Was it the same with both of them? Like fighting with death?'

'They spur each other on. That's probably why they do it together. Like dogs in a pack.'

'And the third one, the boy?'

'He was there to learn.'

They have passed the Cycads sign. Time is almost up.

'If they had been white you wouldn't talk about them in this way,' he says. 'If they had been white thugs from Despatch, for instance.'

'Wouldn't I?'

'No, you wouldn't. I am not blaming you, that is not the point. But it is something new you are talking about. Slavery. They want you for their slave.'

'Not slavery. Subjection. Subjugation.'

He shakes his head. 'It's too much, Lucy. Sell up. Sell the farm to Petrus and come away.'

'No.'

That is where the conversation ends. But Lucy's words echo in his mind. *Covered in blood.* What does she mean? Was he right after all when he dreamt of a bed of blood, a bath of blood?

They do rape. He thinks of the three visitors driving away in the not-too-old Toyota, the back seat piled with household goods, their penises, their weapons, tucked warm and satisfied between their legs – *purring* is the word that comes to him. They must have had every reason to be pleased with their afternoon's work; they must have felt happy in their vocation.

He remembers, as a child, poring over the word *rape* in newspaper reports, trying to puzzle out what exactly it meant,

159

wondering what the letter *p*, usually so gentle, was doing in the middle of a word held in such horror that no one would utter it aloud. In an art-book in the library there was a painting called *The Rape of the Sabine Women*: men on horseback in skimpy Roman armour, women in gauze veils flinging their arms in the air and wailing. What had all this attitudinizing to do with what he suspected rape to be: the man lying on top of the woman and pushing himself into her?

He thinks of Byron. Among the legions of countesses and kitchenmaids Byron pushed himself into there were no doubt those who called it rape. But none surely had cause to fear that the session would end with her throat being slit. From where he stands, from where Lucy stands, Byron looks very old-fashioned indeed.

Lucy was frightened, frightened near to death. Her voice choked, she could not breathe, her limbs went numb. *This is not happening*, she said to herself as the men forced her down; *it is just a dream, a nightmare*. While the men, for their part, drank up her fear, revelled in it, did all they could to hurt her, to menace her, to heighten her terror. *Call your dogs!* they said to her. *Go on, call your dogs! No dogs? Then let us show you dogs!*

You don't understand, you weren't there, says Bev Shaw. Well, she is mistaken. Lucy's intuition is right after all: he does understand; he can, if he concentrates, if he loses himself, be there, be the men, inhabit them, fill them with the ghost of himself. The question is, does he have it in him to be the woman?

From the solitude of his room he writes his daughter a letter:

'Dearest Lucy, With all the love in the world, I must say the following. You are on the brink of a dangerous error. You wish to humble yourself before history. But the road you are following is the wrong one. It will strip you of all honour; you will not be able to live with yourself. I plead with you, listen to me.

'Your father.'

Half an hour later an envelope is pushed under his door. 'Dear David, You have not been listening to me. I am not the person you know. I am a dead person and I do not know yet what will bring me back to life. All I know is that I cannot go away.

'You do not see this, and I do not know what more I can do to make you see. It is as if you have chosen deliberately to sit in a corner where the rays of the sun do not shine. I think of you as one of the three chimpanzees, the one with his paws over his eyes.

'Yes, the road I am following may be the wrong one. But if I leave the farm now I will leave defeated, and will taste that defeat for the rest of my life.

'I cannot be a child for ever. You cannot be a father for ever. I know you mean well, but you are not the guide I need, not at this time.

'Yours, Lucy.'

That is their exchange; that is Lucy's last word.

The business of dog-killing is over for the day, the black bags are piled at the door, each with a body and a soul inside. He and Bev Shaw lie each other's arms on the floor of the surgery. In half an hour Bev will go back to her Bill and he will begin loading the bags.

'You have never told me about your first wife,' says Bev Shaw. 'Lucy doesn't speak about her either.'

'Lucy's mother was Dutch. She must have told you that. Evelina. Evie. After the divorce she went back to Holland. Later she remarried. Lucy didn't get on with the new stepfather. She asked to return to South Africa.'

'So she chose you.'

'In a sense. She also chose a certain surround, a certain horizon. Now I am trying to get her to leave again, if only for a break. She has family in Holland, friends. Holland may not be the most exciting of places to live, but at least it doesn't breed nightmares.'

'And?'

He shrugs. 'Lucy isn't inclined, for the present, to heed any advice I give. She says I am not a good guide.'

'But you were a teacher.'

'Of the most incidental kind. Teaching was never a vocation for me. Certainly I never aspired to teach people how to live. I was what used to be called a scholar. I wrote books about dead people. That was where my heart was. I taught only to make a living.'

She waits for more, but he is not in the mood to go on.

The sun is going down, it is getting cold. They have not made love; they have in effect ceased to pretend that that is what they do together.

In his head Byron, alone on the stage, draws a breath to sing. He is on the point of setting off for Greece. At the age of thirty-five he has begun to understand that life is precious.

Sunt lacrimae rerum, et mentem mortalia tangunt: those will be Byron's words, he is sure of it. As for the music, it hovers somewhere on the horizon, it has not come yet.

'You mustn't worry,' says Bev Shaw. Her head is against his chest: presumably she can hear his heart, with whose beat the hexameter keeps step. 'Bill and I will look after her. We'll go often to the farm. And there's Petrus. Petrus will keep an eye out.'

'Fatherly Petrus.'

'Yes.'

'Lucy says I can't go on being a father for ever. I can't imagine, in this life, not being Lucy's father.'

She runs her fingers through the stubble of his hair. 'It will be all right,' she whispers. 'You will see.'

NINETEEN

THE HOUSE IS part of a development that must, fifteen or twenty years ago, when it was new, have seemed rather bleak, but has since been improved with grassed sidewalks, trees, and creepers that spill over the vibracrete walls. No. 8 Rustholme Crescent has a painted garden gate and an answerphone.

He presses the button. A youthful voice speaks: 'Hello?'

'I'm looking for Mr Isaacs. My name is Lurie.'

'He's not home yet.'

'When do you expect him?'

'Now-now.' A buzz; the latch clicks; he pushes the gate open.

The path leads to the front door, where a slim girl stands watching him. She is dressed in school uniform: marine-blue tunic, white knee-length stockings, open-necked shirt. She has Melanie's eyes, Melanie's wide cheekbones, Melanie's dark hair; she is, if anything, more beautiful. The younger sister Melanie spoke of, whose name he cannot for the moment recollect.

'Good afternoon. When do you expect your father home?'

'School comes out at three, but he usually stays late. It's all right, you can come inside.'

She holds the door open for him, flattening herself as he passes. She is eating a slice of cake, which she holds daintily between two fingers. There are crumbs on her upper lip. He has an urge to reach out, brush them off; at the same instant the memory of her sister comes over him in a hot wave. *God save me*, he thinks – *what am I doing here?*

'You can sit down if you like.'

He sits down. The furniture gleams, the room is oppressively neat.

'What's your name?' he asks.

'Desiree.'

Desiree: now he remembers. Melanie the firstborn, the dark one, then Desiree, the desired one. Surely they tempted the gods by giving her a name like that!

'My name is David Lurie.' He watches her closely, but she gives no sign of recognition. 'I'm from Cape Town.'

'My sister is in Cape Town. She's a student.'

He nods. He does not say, I know your sister, know her well. But he thinks: fruit of the same tree, down probably to the most intimate detail. Yet with differences: different pulsings of the blood, different urgencies of passion. The two of them in the same bed: an experience fit for a king.

He shivers lightly, looks at his watch. 'Do you know what, Desiree? I think I will try to catch your father at his school, if you can tell me how to get there.'

The school is of a piece with the housing estate: a low building in face-brick with steel windows and an asbestos roof, set in a dusty quadrangle fenced with barbed wire. F.S. MARAIS says the writing on the one entrance pillar, MIDDLE SCHOOL says the writing on the other.

The grounds are deserted. He wanders around until he comes upon a sign reading OFFICE. Inside sits a plump middle-aged secretary doing her nails. 'I'm looking for Mr Isaacs,' he says.

'Mr Isaacs!' she calls: 'Here's a visitor for you!' She turns to him. 'Just go in.'

Isaacs, behind his desk, half-rises, pauses, regards him in a puzzled way.

'Do you remember me? David Lurie, from Cape Town.'

'Oh,' says Isaacs, and sits down again. He is wearing the same overlarge suit: his neck vanishes into the jacket, from which he peers out like a sharp-beaked bird caught in a sack. The windows are closed, there is a smell of stale smoke.

'If you don't want to see me I'll leave at once,' he says.

'No,' says Isaacs. 'Sit. I'm just checking attendances. Do you mind if I finish first?'

'Please.'

There is a framed picture on the desk. From where he sits he cannot see it, but he knows what it will be: Melanie and Desiree, apples of their father's eye, with the mother who bore them.

'So,' says Isaacs, closing the last register. 'To what do I owe this pleasure?'

He had expected to be tense, but in fact finds himself quite calm.

'After Melanie lodged her complaint,' he says, 'the university held an official inquiry. As a result I resigned my post. That is the history; you must be aware of it.'

Isaacs stares at him quizzically, giving away nothing.

'Since then I have been at a loose end. I was passing through George today, and I thought I might stop and speak to you. I remember our last meeting as being . . . heated. But I thought I would drop in anyway, and say what is on my heart.'

That much is true. He does want to speak his heart. The question is, what is on his heart?

Isaacs has a cheap Bic pen in his hand. He runs his fingers down the shaft, inverts it, runs his fingers down the shaft, over and over, in a motion that is mechanical rather than impatient.

He continues. 'You have heard Melanie's side of the story. I would like to give you mine, if you are prepared to hear it.

'It began without premeditation on my part. It began as an adventure, one of those sudden little adventures that men of a certain kind have, that I have, that keep me going. Excuse me for talking in this way. I am trying to be frank.

'In Melanie's case, however, something unexpected happened. I think of it as a fire. She struck up a fire in me.'

He pauses. The pen continues its dance. *A sudden little adventure. Men of a certain kind.* Does the man behind the desk have adventures? The more he sees of him the more he doubts it. He would not be surprised if Isaacs were something in the church, a deacon or a server, whatever a server is.

'A fire: what is remarkable about that? If a fire goes out, you strike a match and start another one. That is how I used to think. Yet in the olden days people worshipped fire. They thought twice before letting a flame die, a flame-god. It was that kind of flame your daughter kindled in me. Not hot enough to burn me up, but real: real fire.'

Burned – burnt – burnt up.

The pen has stopped moving. 'Mr Lurie,' says the girl's father, and there is a crooked, pained smile on his face, 'I ask myself what on earth you think you are up to, coming to my school and telling me stories – '

'I'm sorry, it's outrageous, I know. That's the end. That's all I wanted to say, in self-defence. How is Melanie?'

'Melanie is well, since you ask. She phones every week. She has resumed her studies, they gave her a special dispensation to do that, I'm sure you can understand, under the circumstances. She is going on with theatre work in her spare time, and doing well. So Melanie is all right. What about you? What are your plans now that you have left the profession?'

'I have a daughter myself, you will be interested to hear. She owns a farm; I expect to spend some of my time with her, helping

166

out. Also I have a book to complete, a sort of book. One way or another I will keep myself busy.'

He pauses. Isaacs is regarding him with what strikes him as piercing attention.

'So,' says Isaacs softly, and the word leaves his lips like a sigh: 'how are the mighty fallen!'

Fallen? Yes, there has been a fall, no doubt about that. But *mighty*? Does *mighty* describe him? He thinks of himself as obscure and growing obscurer. A figure from the margins of history.

'Perhaps it does us good', he says, 'to have a fall every now and then. As long as we don't break.'

'Good. Good. Good,' says Isaacs, still fixing him with that intent look. For the first time he detects a trace of Melanie in him: a shapeliness of the mouth and lips. On an impulse he reaches across the desk, tries to shake the man's hand, ends up by stroking the back of it. Cool, hairless skin.

'Mr Lurie,' says Isaacs: 'is there something else you want to tell me, besides the story of yourself and Melanie? You mentioned there was something on your heart.'

'On my heart? No. No, I just stopped by to find out how Melanie was.' He rises. 'Thank you for seeing me, I appreciate it.' He reaches out a hand, straightforwardly this time. 'Goodbye.'

'Goodbye.'

He is at the door – he is, in fact, in the outer office, which is now empty – when Isaacs calls out: 'Mr Lurie! Just a minute!'

He returns.

'What are your plans for the evening?'

'This evening? I've checked in at a hotel. I have no plans.'

'Come and have a meal with us. Come for dinner.'

'I don't think your wife would welcome that.'

'Perhaps. Perhaps not. Come anyway. Break bread with us. We eat at seven. Let me write down the address for you.'

'You don't need to do that. I have been to your home already, and met your daughter. It was she who directed me here.'

Isaacs does not bat an eyelid. 'Good,' he says.

The front door is opened by Isaacs himself. 'Come in, come in,' he says, and ushers him into the living-room. Of the wife there is no sign, nor of the second daughter.

'I brought an offering,' he says, and holds out a bottle of wine.

Isaacs thanks him, but seems unsure what to do with the wine. 'Can I give you some? I'll just go and open it.' He leaves the room; there is a whispering in the kitchen. He comes back. 'We seem to have lost the corkscrew. But Dezzy will borrow from the neighbours.'

They are teetotal, clearly. He should have thought of that. A tight little petit-bourgeois household, frugal, prudent. The car washed, the lawn mowed, savings in the bank. All their resources concentrated on launching the two jewel daughters into the future: clever Melanie, with her theatrical ambitions; Desiree, the beauty.

He remembers Melanie, on the first evening of their closer acquaintance, sitting beside him on the sofa drinking the coffee with the shot-glass of whisky in it that was intended to – the word comes up reluctantly – *lubricate* her. Her trim little body; her sexy clothes; her eyes gleaming with excitement. Stepping out in the forest where the wild wolf prowls.

Desiree the beauty enters with the bottle and a corkscrew. As she crosses the floor towards them she hesitates an instant, conscious that a greeting is owed. 'Pa?' she murmurs with a hint of confusion, holding out the bottle.

So: she has found out who he is. They have discussed him, had a tussle over him perhaps: the unwanted visitor, the man whose name is darkness.

Her father has trapped her hand in his. 'Desiree,' he says, 'this is Mr Lurie.'

'Hello, Desiree.'

The hair that had screened her face is tossed back. She meets his gaze, still embarrassed, but stronger now that she is under her father's wing. 'Hello,' she murmurs; and he thinks, *My God, my God!*

As for her, she cannot hide from him what is passing through her mind: *So this is the man my sister has been naked with! So this is the man she has done it with! This old man!*

There is a separate little dining-room, with a hatch to the kitchen. Four places are set with the best cutlery; candles are burning. 'Sit, sit!' says Isaacs. Still no sign of his wife. 'Excuse me a moment.' Isaacs disappears into the kitchen. He is left facing Desiree across the table. She hangs her head, no longer so brave.

Then they return, the two parents together. He stands up. 'You haven't met my wife. Doreen, our guest, Mr Lurie.'

'I am grateful to you for receiving me in your home, Mrs Isaacs.'

Mrs Isaacs is a short woman, growing dumpy in middle age, with bowed legs that give her a faintly rolling walk. But he can see where the sisters get their looks. A real beauty she must have been in her day.

Her features remain stiff, she avoids his eye, but she does give the slightest of nods. Obedient; a good wife and helpmeet. *And ye shall be as one flesh.* Will the daughters take after her?

'Desiree,' she commands, 'come and help carry.'

Gratefully the child tumbles out of her chair.

'Mr Isaacs, I am just causing upset in your home,' he says. 'It was kind of you to invite me, I appreciate it, but it is better that I leave.'

Isaacs gives a smile in which, to his surprise, there is a hint of gaiety. 'Sit down, sit down! We'll be all right! We will do it!' He leans closer. 'You have to be strong!'

Then Desiree and her mother are back bearing dishes: chicken in a bubbling tomato stew that gives off aromas of ginger and cumin, rice, an array of salads and pickles. Just the kind of food he most missed, living with Lucy.

The bottle of wine is set before him, and a solitary wine glass.

'Am I the only one drinking?' he says.

'Please,' says Isaacs. 'Go ahead.'

He pours a glass. He does not like sweet wines, he bought the Late Harvest imagining it would be to their taste. Well, so much the worse for him.

There remains the prayer to get through. The Isaacs take hands; there is nothing for it but to stretch out his hands too, left to the girl's father, right to her mother. 'For what we are about to receive, may the Lord make us truly grateful,' says Isaacs. 'Amen,' say his wife and daughter; and he, David Lurie, mumbles 'Amen' too and lets go the two hands, the father's cool as silk, the mother's small, fleshy, warm from her labours.

Mrs Isaacs dishes up. 'Mind, it's hot,' she says as she passes his plate. Those are her only words to him.

During the meal he tries to be a good guest, to talk entertainingly, to fill the silences. He talks about Lucy, about the boarding kennels, about her bee-keeping and her horticultural projects, about his Saturday morning stints at the market. He glosses over the attack, mentioning only that his car was stolen. He talks about the Animal Welfare League, but not about the incinerator in the hospital grounds or his stolen afternoons with Bev Shaw.

Stitched together in this way, the story unrolls without shadows. Country life in all its idiot simplicity. How he wishes it could be true! He is tired of shadows, of complications, of complicated people. He loves his daughter, but there are times when he wishes she were a simpler being: simpler, neater. The man who raped her, the leader of the gang, was like that. Like a blade cutting the wind.

He has a vision of himself stretched out on an operating table. A scalpel flashes; from throat to groin he is laid open; he sees it all yet feels no pain. A surgeon, bearded, bends over him, frowning. *What is all this stuff?* growls the surgeon. He pokes at the gall bladder. *What is this?* He cuts it out, tosses it aside. He pokes at the heart. *What is this?*

'Your daughter – does she run her farm all alone?' asks Isaacs.

'She has a man who helps sometimes. Petrus. An African.' And he talks about Petrus, solid, dependable Petrus, with his two wives and his moderate ambitions.

He is less hungry than he thought he would be. Conversation flags, but somehow they get through the meal. Desiree excuses herself, goes off to do her homework. Mrs Isaacs clears the table.

'I should be leaving,' he says. 'I am due to make an early start tomorrow.'

'Wait, stay a moment,' says Isaacs.

They are alone. He can prevaricate no longer.

'About Melanie,' he says.

'Yes?'

'One word more, then I am finished. It could have turned out differently, I believe, between the two of us, despite our ages. But there was something I failed to supply, something' – he hunts for the word – 'lyrical. I lack the lyrical. I manage love too well. Even when I burn I don't sing, if you understand me. For which I am sorry. I am sorry for what I took your daughter through. You have a wonderful family. I apologize for the grief I have caused you and Mrs Isaacs. I ask for your pardon.'

Wonderful is not right. Better would be *exemplary*.

'So,' says Isaacs, 'at last you have apologized. I wondered when it was coming.' He ponders. He has not taken his seat; now he begins to pace up and down. 'You are sorry. You lacked the lyrical, you say. If you had had the lyrical, we would not be where we are today. But I say to myself, we are all sorry when we are found out. Then we are very sorry. The question is not, are we sorry? The question is, what lesson have we learned? The question is, what are we going to do now that we are sorry?'

He is about to reply, but Isaacs raises a hand. 'May I pronounce the word *God* in your hearing? You are not one of those people who get upset when they hear God's name? The question is, what does God want from you, besides being very sorry? Have you any ideas, Mr Lurie?'

Though distracted by Isaacs's back-and-forth, he tries to pick his words carefully. 'Normally I would say', he says, 'that after a certain age one is too old to learn lessons. One can only be punished and punished. But perhaps that is not true, not always. I wait to see. As for God, I am not a believer, so I will have to translate what you call God and God's wishes into my own terms. In my own terms, I am being punished for what happened between myself and your daughter. I am sunk into a state of disgrace from which it will not be easy to lift myself. It is not a punishment I have refused. I do not murmur against it. On the contrary, I am living it out from day to day, trying to accept disgrace as my state of being. Is it enough for God, do you think, that I live in disgrace without term?'

'I don't know, Mr Lurie. Normally I would say, don't ask me, ask God. But since you don't pray, you have no way to ask God. So God must find his own means of telling you. Why do you think you are here, Mr Lurie?'

He is silent.

'I will tell you. You were passing through George, and it occurred to you that your student's family was from George, and you thought to yourself, *Why not?* You didn't plan on it, yet now you find yourself in our home. That must come as a surprise to you. Am I right?'

'Not quite. I was not telling the truth. I was not just passing through. I came to George for one reason alone: to speak to you. I had been thinking about it for some time.'

'Yes, you came to speak to me, you say, but why me? I'm easy to speak to, too easy. All the children at my school know that. With Isaacs you get off easy – that is what they say.' He is smiling again, the same crooked smile as before. 'So who did you really come to speak to?'

Now he is sure of it: he does not like this man, does not like his tricks.

He rises, blunders through the empty dining-room and down the passage. From behind a half-closed door he hears low voices. He pushes the door open. Sitting on the bed are Desiree and her mother, doing something with a skein of wool. Astonished at the sight of him, they fall silent.

With careful ceremony he gets to his knees and touches his forehead to the floor.

Is that enough? he thinks. Will that do? If not, what more?

He raises his head. The two of them are still sitting there, frozen. He meets the mother's eyes, then the daughter's, and again the current leaps, the current of desire.

He gets to his feet, a little more creakily than he would have wished. 'Good night,' he says. 'Thank you for your kindness. Thank you for the meal.'

At eleven o'clock there is a call for him in his hotel room. It is Isaacs. 'I am phoning to wish you strength for the future.' A pause. 'There is a question I never got to ask, Mr Lurie. You are not hoping for us to intervene on your behalf, are you, with the university?'

'To intervene?'

'Yes. To reinstate you, for instance.'

'The thought never crossed my mind. I have finished with the university.'

'Because the path you are on is one that God has ordained for you. It is not for us to interfere.'

'Understood.'

TWENTY

HE RE-ENTERS Cape Town on the N2. He has been away less than three months, yet in that time the shanty settlements have crossed the highway and spread east of the airport. The stream of cars has to slow down while a child with a stick herds a stray cow off the road. Inexorably, he thinks, the country is coming to the city. Soon there will be cattle again on Rondebosch Common; soon history will have come full circle.

So he is home again. It does not feel like a homecoming. He cannot imagine taking up residence once more in the house on Torrance Road, in the shadow of the university, skulking about like a criminal, dodging old colleagues. He will have to sell the house, move to a flat somewhere cheaper.

His finances are in chaos. He has not paid a bill since he left. He is living on credit; any day now his credit is going to dry up.

The end of roaming. What comes after the end of roaming? He sees himself, white-haired, stooped, shuffling to the corner shop to buy his half-litre of milk and half-loaf of bread; he sees himself sitting blankly at a desk in a room full of yellowing papers, waiting for the afternoon to peter out so that he can cook his evening meal and go to bed. The life of a superannuated scholar, without hope, without prospect: is that what he is prepared to settle for?

He unlocks the front gate. The garden is overgrown, the

mailbox stuffed tight with flyers, advertisements. Though well fortified by most standards, the house has stood empty for months: too much to hope for that it will not have been visited. And indeed, from the moment he opens the front door and smells the air he knows there is something wrong. His heart begins to thud with a sick excitement.

There is no sound. Whoever was here is gone. But how did they get in? Tiptoeing from room to room, he soon finds out. The bars over one of the back windows have been torn out of the wall and folded back, the windowpanes smashed, leaving enough of a hole for a child or even a small man to climb through. A mat of leaves and sand, blown in by the wind, has caked on the floor.

He wanders through the house taking a census of his losses. His bedroom has been ransacked, the cupboards yawn bare. His sound equipment is gone, his tapes and records, his computer equipment. In his study the desk and filing cabinet have been broken open; papers are scattered everywhere. The kitchen has been thoroughly stripped: cutlery, crockery, smaller appliances. His liquor store is gone. Even the cupboard that had held canned food is empty.

No ordinary burglary. A raiding party moving in, cleaning out the site, retreating laden with bags, boxes, suitcases. Booty; war reparations; another incident in the great campaign of redistribution. Who is at this moment wearing his shoes? Have Beethoven and Janáček found homes for themselves or have they been tossed out on the rubbish heap?

From the bathroom comes a bad smell. A pigeon, trapped in the house, has expired in the basin. Gingerly he lifts the mess of bones and feathers into a plastic packet and ties it shut.

The lights are cut off, the telephone is dead. Unless he does something about it he will spend the night in the dark. But he is too depressed to act. Let it all go to hell, he thinks, and sinks into a chair and closes his eyes.

As dusk settles he rouses himself and leaves the house. The first stars are out. Through empty streets, through gardens heavy with the scent of verbena and jonquil, he makes his way to the university campus.

He still has his keys to the Communications Building. A good hour to come haunting: the corridors are deserted. He takes the lift to his office on the fifth floor. The name-tag on his door has been removed. DR S. OTTO, reads the new tag. From under the door comes a faint light.

He knocks. No sound. He unlocks the door and enters.

The room has been transformed. His books and pictures are gone, leaving the walls bare save for a poster-size blowup of a comic-book panel: Superman hanging his head as he is berated by Lois Lane.

Behind the computer, in the half-light, sits a young man he has not seen before. The young man frowns. 'Who are you?' he asks.

'I'm David Lurie.'

'Yes? And?'

'I've come to pick up my mail. This used to be my office.' *In the past*, he almost adds.

'Oh, right, David Lurie. Sorry, I wasn't thinking. I put it all in a box. And some other stuff of yours that I found.' He waves. 'Over there.'

'And my books?'

'They are all downstairs in the storage room.'

He picks up the box. 'Thank you,' he says.

'No problem,' says young Dr Otto. 'Can you manage that?'

He takes the heavy box across to the library, intending to sort through his mail. But when he reaches the access barrier the machine will no longer accept his card. He has to do his sorting on a bench in the lobby.

*

He is too restless to sleep. At dawn he heads for the mountainside and sets off on a long walk. It has rained, the streams are in spate. He breathes in the heady scent of pine. As of today he is a free man, with duties to no one but himself. Time lies before him to spend as he wishes. The feeling is unsettling, but he presumes he will get used to it.

His spell with Lucy has not turned him into a country person. Nonetheless, there are things he misses – the duck family, for instance: Mother Duck tacking about on the surface of the dam, her chest puffed out with pride, while Eenie, Meenie, Minie and Mo paddle busily behind, confident that as long as she is there they are safe from all harm.

As for the dogs, he does not want to think about them. From Monday onward the dogs released from life within the walls of the clinic will be tossed into the fire unmarked, unmourned. For that betrayal, will he ever be forgiven?

He visits the bank, takes a load of washing to the laundry. In the little shop where for years he has bought his coffee the assistant pretends not to recognize him. His neighbour, watering her garden, studiously keeps her back turned.

He thinks of William Wordsworth on his first stay in London, visiting the pantomime, seeing Jack the Giant Killer blithely striding the stage, flourishing his sword, protected by the word *Invisible* written on his chest.

In the evening he calls Lucy from a public telephone. 'I thought I'd phone in case you were worried about me,' he says. 'I'm fine. I'll take a while to settle down, I suspect. I rattle about in the house like a pea in a bottle. I miss the ducks.'

He does not mention the raid on the house. What is the good of burdening Lucy with his troubles?

'And Petrus?' he asks. 'Has Petrus been looking after you, or is he still wrapped up in his housebuilding?'

'Petrus has been helping out. Everyone has been helpful.'

'Well, I can come back any time you need me. You have only to say the word.'

'Thank you, David. Not at present, perhaps, but one of these days.'

Who would have guessed, when his child was born, that in time he would come crawling to her asking to be taken in?

Shopping at the supermarket, he finds himself in a queue behind Elaine Winter, chair of his onetime department. She has a whole trolleyful of purchases, he a mere handbasket. Nervously she returns his greeting.

'And how is the department getting on without me?' he asks as cheerily as he can.

Very well indeed – that would be the frankest answer: *We are getting on very well without you.* But she is too polite to say the words. 'Oh, struggling along as usual,' she replies vaguely.

'Have you been able to do any hiring?'

'We have taken on one new person, on a contract basis. A young man.'

I have met him, he might respond. *A right little prick,* he might add. But he too is well brought up. 'What is his specialism?' he inquires instead.

'Applied language studies. He is in language learning.'

So much for the poets, so much for the dead masters. Who have not, he must say, guided him well. *Aliter*, to whom he has not listened well.

The woman ahead of them in the queue is taking her time to pay. There is still room for Elaine to ask the next question, which should be, *And how are you getting on, David?*, and for him to respond, *Very well, Elaine, very well.*

'Wouldn't you like to go ahead of me?' she suggests instead, gesturing toward his basket. 'You have so little.'

'Wouldn't dream of it, Elaine,' he replies, then takes some pleasure in observing as she unloads her purchases on to the counter: not only the bread and butter items but the little treats that a woman living alone awards herself – full cream ice cream (real almonds, real raisins), imported Italian cookies, chocolate bars – as well as a pack of sanitary napkins.

She pays by credit card. From the far side of the barrier she gives him a farewell wave. Her relief is palpable. 'Goodbye!' he calls over the cashier's head. 'Give my regards to everyone!' She does not look back.

As first conceived, the opera had had at its centre Lord Byron and his mistress the Contessa Guiccioli. Trapped in the Villa Guiccioli in the stifling summer heat of Ravenna, spied on by Teresa's jealous husband, the two would roam through the gloomy drawing-rooms singing of their baulked passion. Teresa feels herself to be a prisoner; she smoulders with resentment and nags Byron to bear her away to another life. As for Byron, he is full of doubts, though too prudent to voice them. Their early ecstasies will, he suspects, never be repeated. His life is becalmed; obscurely he has begun to long for a quiet retirement; failing that, for apotheosis, for death. Teresa's soaring arias ignite no spark in him; his own vocal line, dark, convoluted, goes past, through, over her.

That is how he had conceived it: as a chamber-play about love and death, with a passionate young woman and a once passionate but now less than passionate older man; as an action with a complex, restless music behind it, sung in an English that tugs continually toward an imagined Italian.

Formally speaking, the conception is not a bad one. The characters balance one another well: the trapped couple, the discarded mistress hammering at the windows, the jealous husband. The villa too, with Byron's pet monkeys hanging languidly from the chandeliers and peacocks fussing back and forth among the ornate Neapolitan furniture, has the right mix of timelessness and decay.

Yet, first on Lucy's farm and now again here, the project has failed to engage the core of him. There is something misconceived about it, something that does not come from the heart. A woman complaining to the stars that the spying of the servants forces her and her lover to relieve their desires in a broom-closet – who cares? He can find words for Byron, but the Teresa that history has bequeathed him – young, greedy, wilful, petulant – does not match up to the music he has dreamed of, music whose harmonies, lushly autumnal yet edged with irony, he hears shadowed in his inner ear.

He tries another track. Abandoning the pages of notes he has written, abandoning the pert, precocious newlywed with her captive English Milord, he tries to pick Teresa up in middle age. The new Teresa is a dumpy little widow installed in the Villa Gamba with her aged father, running the household, holding the purse-strings tight, keeping an eye out that the servants do not steal the sugar. Byron, in the new version, is long dead; Teresa's sole remaining claim to immortality, and the solace of her lonely nights, is the chestful of letters and memorabilia she keeps under her bed, what she calls her *reliquie*, which her grand-nieces are meant to open after her death and peruse with awe.

Is this the heroine he has been seeking all the time? Will an older Teresa engage his heart as his heart is now?

The passage of time has not treated Teresa kindly. With her heavy bust, her stocky trunk, her abbreviated legs, she looks more like a peasant, a *contadina*, than an aristocrat. The complexion that Byron once so admired has turned hectic; in summer she is overtaken with attacks of asthma that leave her heaving for breath.

In the letters he wrote to her Byron calls her *My friend*, then *My love*, then *My love for ever*. But there are rival letters in existence, letters she cannot reach and set fire to. In these letters, addressed to his English friends, Byron lists her flippantly among his Italian conquests, makes jokes about her husband, alludes to women from her circle with whom he has slept. In the years since Byron's death, his friends have written one memoir after another, drawing upon his letters. After conquering the young Teresa from her husband, runs the story they tell, Byron soon grew bored with her; he found her empty-headed; he stayed with her only out of dutifulness; it was in order to escape her that he sailed off to Greece and to his death.

Their libels hurt her to the quick. Her years with Byron constitute the apex of her life. Byron's love is all that sets her apart. Without him she is nothing: a woman past her prime, without prospects, living out her days in a dull provincial town, exchanging visits with women-friends, massaging her father's legs when they give him pain, sleeping alone.

Can he find it in his heart to love this plain, ordinary woman? Can he love her enough to write a music for her? If he cannot, what is left for him?

He comes back to what must now be the opening scene. The tail end of yet another sultry day. Teresa stands at a second-floor window in her father's house, looking out over the marshes and pine-scrub of the Romagna toward the sun glinting on the Adriatic. The end of the prelude; a hush; she takes a breath. *Mio Byron*, she sings, her voice throbbing with sadness. A lone clarinet answers, tails off, falls silent. *Mio Byron*, she calls again, more strongly.

Where is he, her Byron? Byron is lost, that is the answer. Byron wanders among the shades. And she is lost too, the Teresa he loved, the girl of nineteen with the blonde ringlets who gave herself up with such joy to the imperious Englishman, and afterwards stroked his brow as he lay on her naked breast, breathing deeply, slumbering after his great passion.

Mio Byron, she sings a third time; and from somewhere, from the caverns of the underworld, a voice sings back, wavering and disembodied, the voice of a ghost, the voice of Byron. *Where are you?* he sings; and then a word she does not want to hear: *secca*, dry. *It has dried up, the source of everything.*

So faint, so faltering is the voice of Byron that Teresa has to sing his words back to him, helping him along breath by breath, drawing him back to life: her child, her boy. *I am here*, she sings, supporting him, saving him from going down. *I am your source. Do you remember how together we visited the spring of Arquà? Together, you and I. I was your Laura. Do you remember?*

That is how it must be from here on: Teresa giving voice to her lover, and he, the man in the ransacked house, giving voice to Teresa. The halt helping the lame, for want of better.

Working as swiftly as he can, holding tight to Teresa, he tries to sketch out the opening pages of a libretto. Get the words down on paper, he tells himself. Once that is done it will all be easier. Then there will be time to search through the masters – through Gluck, for instance – lifting melodies, perhaps – who knows? – lifting ideas too.

But by steps, as he begins to live his days more fully with Teresa and the dead Byron, it becomes clear that purloined songs will not be good enough, that the two will demand a music of their own. And, astonishingly, in dribs and drabs, the music comes. Sometimes the contour of a phrase occurs to him before he has a hint of what the words themselves will be; sometimes the words call forth the cadence; sometimes the shade of a melody, having hovered for days on the edge of hearing, unfolds and blessedly reveals itself. As the action begins to unwind, furthermore, it calls up of its own accord modulations and transitions that he feels in his blood even when he has not the musical resources to realize them.

At the piano he sets to work piecing together and writing down the beginnings of a score. But there is something about the sound of the piano that hinders him: too rounded, too physical, too rich. From the attic, from a crate full of old books and toys of Lucy's, he recovers the odd little seven-stringed banjo that he bought for her on the streets of KwaMashu when she was a child. With the aid of the banjo he begins to notate the music that Teresa, now mournful, now angry, will sing to her dead lover, and that pale-voiced Byron will sing back to her from the land of the shades.

The deeper he follows the Contessa into her underworld, singing her words for her or humming her vocal line, the more inseparable from her, to his surprise, becomes the silly plink-plonk of the toy banjo. The lush arias he had dreamed of giving her he quietly abandons; from there it is but a short step to putting the instrument into her hands. Instead of stalking the stage, Teresa now sits staring out over the marshes toward the gates of hell, cradling the mandolin on which she accompanies herself in her lyric flights; while to one side a discreet trio in knee-breeches (cello, flute, bassoon) fill in the entr'actes or comment sparingly between stanzas.

Seated at his own desk looking out on the overgrown garden, he marvels at what the little banjo is teaching him. Six months ago he had thought his own ghostly place in *Byron in Italy* would be somewhere between Teresa's and Byron's: between a yearning to prolong the summer of the passionate body and a reluctant recall from the long sleep of oblivion. But he was wrong. It is not the erotic that is calling to him after all, nor the elegiac, but the comic. He is in the opera neither as Teresa nor as Byron nor even as some blending of the two: he is held in the music itself, in the flat, tinny slap of the banjo strings, the voice that strains to soar away from the ludicrous instrument but is continually reined back, like a fish on a line.

So this is art, he thinks, and this is how it does its work! How strange! How fascinating!

He spends whole days in the grip of Byron and Teresa, living on black coffee and breakfast cereal. The refrigerator is empty, his bed is unmade; leaves chase across the floor from the broken window. No matter, he thinks: let the dead bury their dead.

Out of the poets I learned to love, chants Byron in his cracked monotone, nine syllables on C natural; *but life, I found* (descending chromatically to F), *is another story. Plink-plunk-plonk* go the strings of the banjo. *Why, O why do you speak like that?* sings Teresa in a long reproachful arc. *Plunk-plink-plonk* go the strings.

She wants to be loved, Teresa, to be loved immortally; she wants to be raised to the company of the Lauras and Floras of yore. And Byron? Byron will be faithful unto death, but that is all he promises. *Let both be tied till one shall have expired.*

My love, sings Teresa, swelling out the fat English monosyllable she learned in the poet's bed. *Plink*, echo the strings. A woman in love, wallowing in love; a cat on a roof, howling; complex proteins swirling in the blood, distending the sexual organs, making the palms sweat and voice thicken as the soul hurls its longings to the skies. That is what Soraya and the others were for: to suck the complex proteins out of his blood like snake-venom, leaving him clear-headed and dry. Teresa in her father's house in Ravenna, to her misfortune, has no one to suck the venom from her. *Come to me, mio Byron*, she cries: *come to me, love me!* And Byron, exiled from life, pale as a ghost, echoes her derisively: *Leave me, leave me, leave me be!*

Years ago, when he lived in Italy, he visited the same forest between Ravenna and the Adriatic coastline where a century and a half before Byron and Teresa used to go riding. Somewhere among the trees must be the spot where the Englishman first lifted the skirts of his eighteen-year-old charmer, bride of another man. He could fly to Venice tomorrow, catch a train to Ravenna, tramp along the old riding-trails, pass by the very place. He is inventing the music (or the music is inventing him) but he is not inventing the history. On those pine-needles Byron had his Teresa – 'timid as a gazelle,' he called her – rumpling her clothes, getting sand into her underwear (the horses standing by all the while, incurious), and from the occasion a passion was born that kept Teresa howling to the moon for the rest of her natural life in a fever that has set him howling too, after his manner.

Teresa leads; page after page he follows. Then one day there emerges from the dark another voice, one he has not heard before, has not counted on hearing. From the words he knows it belongs to Byron's daughter Allegra; but from where inside him does it come? *Why have you left me? Come and fetch me!* calls Allegra. *So hot, so hot, so hot!* she complains in a rhythm of her own that cuts insistently across the voices of the lovers.

To the call of the inconvenient five-year-old there comes no answer. Unlovely, unloved, neglected by her famous father, she has been passed from hand to hand and finally given to the nuns to look after. *So hot, so hot!* she whines from the bed in the convent where she is dying of *la mal'aria. Why have you forgotten me?*

Why will her father not answer? Because he has had enough of life; because he would rather be back where he belongs, on death's other shore, sunk in his old sleep. *My poor little baby!* sings Byron, waveringly, unwillingly, too softly for her to hear. Seated in the shadows to one side, the trio of instrumentalists play the crablike motif, one line going up, the other down, that is Byron's.

TWENTY-ONE

ROSALIND TELEPHONES. 'Lucy says you are back in town. Why haven't you been in touch?' 'I'm not yet fit for society,' he replies. 'Were you ever?' comments Rosalind drily.

They meet in a coffee-shop in Claremont. 'You've lost weight,' she remarks. 'What happened to your ear?' 'It's nothing,' he replies, and will not explain further.

As they talk her gaze keeps drifting back to the misshapen ear. She would shudder, he is sure, if she had to touch it. Not the ministering type. His best memories are still of their first months together: steamy summer nights in Durban, sheets damp with perspiration, Rosalind's long, pale body thrashing this way and that in the throes of a pleasure that was hard to tell from pain. Two sensualists: that was what held them together, while it lasted.

They talk about Lucy, about the farm. 'I thought she had a friend living with her,' says Rosalind. 'Grace.'

'Helen. Helen is back in Johannesburg. I suspect they have broken up for good.'

'Is Lucy safe by herself in that lonely place?'

'No, she isn't safe, she would be mad to feel safe. But she will stay on nevertheless. It has become a point of honour with her.'

'You said you had your car stolen.'

'It was my own fault. I should have been more careful.'

'I forgot to mention: I heard the story of your trial. The inside story. '

'My trial?'

'Your inquiry, your inquest, whatever you call it. I heard you didn't perform well.'

'Oh? How did you hear? I thought it was confidential.'

'That doesn't matter. I heard you didn't make a good impression. You were too stiff and defensive.'

'I wasn't trying to make an impression. I was standing up for a principle.'

'That may be so, David, but surely you know by now that trials are not about principles, they are about how well you put yourself across. According to my source, you came across badly. What was the principle you were standing up for?'

'Freedom of speech. Freedom to remain silent.'

'That sounds very grand. But you were always a great self-deceiver, David. A great deceiver and a great self-deceiver. Are you sure it wasn't just a case of being caught with your pants down?'

He does not rise to the bait.

'Anyway, whatever the principle was, it was too abstruse for your audience. They thought you were just obfuscating. You should have got yourself some coaching beforehand. What are you going to do about money? Did they take away your pension?'

'I'll get back what I put in. I am going to sell the house. It's too big for me.'

'What will you do with your time? Will you look for a job?'

'I don't think so. My hands are full. I'm writing something.'

'A book?'

'An opera, in fact.'

'An opera! Well, that's a new departure. I hope it makes you lots of money. Will you move in with Lucy?'

'The opera is just a hobby, something to dabble at. It won't make money. And no, I won't be moving in with Lucy. It wouldn't be a good idea.'

'Why not? You and she have always got on well together. Has something happened?'

Her questions are intrusive, but Rosalind has never had qualms about being intrusive. 'You shared my bed for ten years,' she once said – 'Why should you have secrets from me?'

'Lucy and I still get on well,' he replies. 'But not well enough to live together.'

'The story of your life.'

'Yes.'

There is silence while they contemplate, from their respective angles, the story of his life.

'I saw your girlfriend,' Rosalind says, changing the subject.

'My girlfriend?'

'Your inamorata. Melanie Isaacs – isn't that her name? She is in a play at the Dock Theatre. Didn't you know? I can see why you fell for her. Big, dark eyes. Cunning little weasel body. Just your type. You must have thought it would be another of your quick flings, your peccadilloes. And now look at you. You have thrown away your life, and for what?'

'My life is not thrown away, Rosalind. Be sensible.'

'But it is! You have lost your job, your name is mud, your friends avoid you, you hide out in Torrance Road like a tortoise afraid to stick its neck out of its shell. People who aren't good enough to tie your shoelaces make jokes about you. Your shirt isn't ironed, God know who gave you that haircut, you've got – ' She arrests her tirade. 'You are going to end up as one of those sad old men who poke around in rubbish bins.'

'I'm going to end up in a hole in the ground,' he says. 'And so are you. So are we all.'

'That's enough, David, I'm upset as it is, I don't want to get into an argument.' She gathers up her packages. 'When you are tired of bread and jam, give me a call and I'll cook you a meal.'

The mention of Melanie Isaacs unsettles him. He has never been given to lingering involvements. When an affair is over, he puts it behind him. But there is something unfinished in the business with Melanie. Deep inside him the smell of her is stored, the smell of a mate. Does she remember his smell too? *Just your type*, said Rosalind, who ought to know. What if their paths cross again, his and Melanie's? Will there be a flash of feeling, a sign that the affair has not run its course?

Yet the very idea of reapplying to Melanie is crazy. Why should she speak to the man condemned as her persecutor? And what will she think of him anyway – the dunce with the funny ear, the uncut hair, the rumpled collar?

The marriage of Cronus and Harmony: unnatural. That was what the trial was set up to punish, once all the fine words were stripped away. On trial for his way of life. For unnatural acts: for broadcasting old seed, tired seed, seed that does not quicken, *contra naturam*. If the old men hog the young women, what will be the future of the species? That, at bottom, was the case for the prosecution. Half of literature is about it: young women struggling to escape from under the weight of old men, for the sake of the species.

He sighs. The young in one another's arms, heedless, engrossed in the sensual music. No country, this, for old men. He seems to be spending a lot of time sighing. Regret: a regrettable note on which to go out.

Until two years ago the Dock Theatre was a cold storage plant where the carcases of pigs and oxen hung waiting to be transported across the seas. Now it is a fashionable entertainment spot. He arrives late, taking his seat just as the lights are dimming. 'A runaway success brought back by popular demand': that is how *Sunset at the Globe Salon* is billed in its new production. The set is more stylish, the direction more professional, there is a new lead actor. Nevertheless, he finds the play, with its crude humour and nakedly political intent, as hard to endure as before.

Melanie has kept her part as Gloria, the novice hairdresser. Wearing a pink caftan over gold lamé tights, her face garishly made up, her hair piled in loops on her head, she totters onstage on high heels. The lines she is given are predictable, but she delivers them with deft timing in a whining *Kaaps* accent. She is altogether more sure of herself than before – in fact, good in the part, positively gifted. Is it possible that in the months he has been away she has grown up, found herself? *Whatever does not kill me makes me stronger.* Perhaps the trial was a trial for her too; perhaps she too has suffered, and come through.

He wishes he could have a sign. If he had a sign he would know what to do. If, for instance, those absurd clothes were to burn off her body in a cold, private flame and she were to stand before him, in a revelation secret to him alone, as naked and as perfect as on that last night in Lucy's old room.

The holidaymakers among whom he is seated, ruddy-faced, comfortable in their heavy flesh, are enjoying the play. They have taken to Melanie-Gloria; they titter at the risqué jokes, laugh uproariously when the characters trade slurs and insults.

Though they are his countrymen, he could not feel more alien among them, more of an impostor. Yet when they laugh at Melanie's lines he cannot resist a flush of pride. *Mine!* he would like to say, turning to them, as if she were his daughter.

Without warning a memory comes back from years ago: of someone he picked up on the N1 outside Trompsburg and gave a ride to, a woman in her twenties travelling alone, a tourist from Germany, sunburnt and dusty. They drove as far as Touws River, checked into a hotel; he fed her, slept with her. He remembers her long, wiry legs; he remembers the softness of her hair, its feather-lightness between his fingers.

In a sudden and soundless eruption, as if he has fallen into a waking dream, a stream of images pours down, images of women he has known on two continents, some from so far away in time that he barely recognizes them. Like leaves blown on the wind, pell-mell, they pass before him. *A fair field full of folk*: hundreds of lives all tangled with his. He holds his breath, willing the vision to continue.

What has happened to them, all those women, all those lives? Are there moments when they too, or some of them, are plunged without warning into the ocean of memory? The German girl: is it possible that at this very instant she is remembering the man who picked her up on the roadside in Africa and spent the night with her?

Enriched: that was the word the newspapers picked on to jeer at. A stupid word to let slip, under the circumstances, yet now, at this moment, he would stand by it. By Melanie, by the girl in Touws River; by Rosalind, Bev Shaw, Soraya: by each of them he was enriched, and by the others too, even the least of them, even the failures. Like a flower blooming in his breast, his heart floods with thankfulness.

Where do moments like this come from? Hypnagogic, no doubt; but what does that explain? If he is being led, then what god is doing the leading?

The play is grinding on. They have come to the point where Melanie gets her broom tangled in the electric cord. A flash of magnesium, and the stage is suddenly plunged into darkness. *'Jesus Christ, jou dom meid!'* screeches the hairdresser.

There are twenty rows of seats between himself and Melanie, but he hopes she can at this moment, across space, smell him, smell his thoughts.

Something raps him lightly on the head, calling him back to the world. A moment later another object flits past and hits the seat in front of him: a spitball of paper the size of a marble. A third hits him in the neck. He is the target, no doubt of that.

He is supposed to turn and glare. *Who did that?* he is supposed to bark. Or else stare stiffly ahead, pretending not to notice.

A fourth pellet strikes his shoulder and bounces into the air. The man in the next seat steals a puzzled glance.

On stage the action has progressed. Sidney the hairdresser is tearing open the fatal envelope and reading aloud the landlord's ultimatum. They have until the end of the month to pay the back rent, failing which the Globe will have to close down. 'What are we going to do?' laments Miriam the hair-washing woman.

'*Sss*,' comes a hiss from behind him, soft enough not to be heard at the front of the house. '*Sss*.'

He turns, and a pellet catches him on the temple. Standing against the back wall is Ryan, the boyfriend with the ear-ring and goatee. Their eyes meet. 'Professor Lurie!' whispers Ryan hoarsely. Outrageous though his behaviour is, he seems quite at ease. There is a little smile on his lips.

The play goes on, but there is around him now a definite flurry of unrest. '*Sss*,' hisses Ryan again. 'Be quiet!' exclaims the woman two seats away, directing herself at him, though he has uttered not a sound.

There are five pairs of knees to fight past ('Excuse me ... Excuse me'), cross looks, angry murmurings, before he can reach the aisle, find his way out, emerge into the windy, moonless night.

There is a sound behind him. He turns. The point of a cigarette glows: Ryan has followed him into the parking lot.

'Are you going to explain yourself?' he snaps. 'Are you going to explain this childish behaviour?'

Ryan draws on his cigarette. 'Only doing you a favour, prof. Didn't you learn your lesson?'

'What was my lesson?'

'Stay with your own kind.'

Your own kind: who is this boy to tell him who his kind are? What does he know of the force that drives the utmost strangers into each other's arms, making them kin, kind, beyond all prudence? *Omnis gens quaecumque se in se perficere vult*. The seed of generation, driven to perfect itself, driving deep into the woman's body, driving to bring the future into being. Drive, driven.

Ryan is speaking. 'Let her alone, man! Melanie will spit in your eye if she sees you.' He drops his cigarette, takes a step closer. Under stars so bright one might think them on fire they face each other. 'Find yourself another life, prof. Believe me.'

He drives back slowly along the Main Road in Green Point. *Spit in your eye*: he had not expected that. His hand on the steering wheel is trembling. The shocks of existence: he must learn to take them more lightly.

The streetwalkers are out in numbers; at a traffic light one of them catches his eye, a tall girl in a minute black leather skirt. *Why not*, he thinks, *on this night of revelations?*

They park in a cul-de-sac on the slopes of Signal Hill. The girl is drunk or perhaps on drugs: he can get nothing coherent out of her. Nonetheless, she does her work on him as well as he could expect. Afterwards she lies with her face in his lap, resting. She is younger than she had seemed under the streetlights, younger even than Melanie. He lays a hand on her head. The trembling has ceased. He feels drowsy, contented; also strangely protective.

So this is all it takes!, he thinks. *How could I ever have forgotten it?*

Not a bad man but not good either. Not cold but not hot, even at his hottest. Not by the measure of Teresa; not even by the measure of Byron. Lacking in fire. Will that be the verdict on him, the verdict of the universe and its all-seeing eye?

The girl stirs, sits up. 'Where are you taking me?' she mumbles.

'I'm taking you back to where I found you.'

TWENTY-TWO

HE STAYS IN contact with Lucy by telephone. In their conversations she is at pains to assure him that all is well on the farm, he to give the impression that he does not doubt her. She is hard at work in the flowerbeds, she tells him, where the spring crop is now in bloom. The kennels are reviving. She has two dogs on full board and hopes of more. Petrus is busy with his house, but not too busy to help out. The Shaws are frequent visitors. No, she does not need money.

But something in Lucy's tone nags at him. He telephones Bev Shaw. 'You are the only person I can ask,' he says. 'How is Lucy, truthfully?'

Bev Shaw is guarded. 'What has she told you?'

'She tells me that everything is fine. But she sounds like a zombie. She sounds as if she is on tranquillizers. Is she?'

Bev Shaw evades the question. However, she says – and she seems to be picking her words carefully – there have been 'developments'.

'What developments?'

'I can't tell you, David. Don't make me. Lucy will have to tell you yourself.'

He calls Lucy. 'I must make a trip to Durban,' he says, lying. 'There is the possibility of a job. May I stop off for a day or two?'

'Has Bev been speaking to you?'

'Bev has nothing to do with it. May I come?'

He flies to Port Elizabeth and hires a car. Two hours later he turns off the road on to the track that leads to the farm, Lucy's farm, Lucy's patch of earth.

Is it his earth too? It does not feel like his earth. Despite the time he has spent here, it feels like a foreign land.

There have been changes. A wire fence, not particularly skilfully erected, now marks the boundary between Lucy's property and Petrus's. On Petrus's side graze a pair of scrawny heifers. Petrus's house has become a reality. Grey and featureless, it stands on an eminence east of the old farmhouse; in the mornings, he guesses, it must cast a long shadow.

Lucy opens the door wearing a shapeless smock that might as well be a nightdress. Her old air of brisk good health is gone. Her complexion is pasty, she has not washed her hair. Without warmth she returns his embrace. 'Come in,' she says. 'I was just making tea.'

They sit together at the kitchen table. She pours tea, passes him a packet of ginger snaps. 'Tell me about the Durban offer,' she says.

'That can wait. I am here, Lucy, because I am concerned about you. Are you all right?'

'I'm pregnant.'

'You are what?'

'I'm pregnant.'

'From whom? From that day?'

'From that day.'

'I don't understand. I thought you took care of it, you and your GP.'

'No.'

'What do you mean, no? You mean you didn't take care of it?'

'I have taken care. I have taken every reasonable care short of what you are hinting at. But I am not having an abortion. That is something I am not prepared to go through with again.'

'I didn't know you felt that way. You never told me you did not believe in abortion. Why should there be a question of abortion anyway? I thought you took Ovral.'

'This has nothing to do with belief. And I never said I took Ovral.'

'You could have told me earlier. Why did you keep it from me?'

'Because I couldn't face one of your eruptions. David, I can't run my life according to whether or not you like what I do. Not any more. You behave as if everything I do is part of the story of your life. You are the main character, I am a minor character who doesn't make an appearance until halfway through. Well, contrary to what you think, people are not divided into major and minor. I am not minor. I have a life of my own, just as important to me as yours is to you, and in my life I am the one who makes the decisions.'

An eruption? Is this not an eruption in its own right? 'That's enough, Lucy,' he says, taking her hand across the table. 'Are you telling me you are going to have the child?'

'Yes.'

'A child from one of those men?'

'Yes.'

'Why?'

'Why? I am a woman, David. Do you think I hate children? Should I choose against the child because of who its father is?'

'It has been known. When are you expecting it?'

'May. The end of May.'

'And your mind is made up?'

'Yes.'

'Very well. This has come as a shock to me, I confess, but I will stand by you, whatever you decide. There is no question about that. Now I am going to take a walk. We can talk again later.'

Why can they not talk now? Because he is shaken. Because there is a risk that he too might erupt.

She is not prepared, she says, to go through with it again. Therefore she has had an abortion before. He would never have guessed it. When could it have been? While she was still living at home? Did Rosalind know, and was he kept in the dark?

The gang of three. Three fathers in one. Rapists rather than robbers, Lucy called them – rapists cum taxgatherers roaming the area, attacking women, indulging their violent pleasures. Well, Lucy was wrong. They were not raping, they were mating. It was not the pleasure principle that ran the show but the testicles, sacs bulging with seed aching to perfect itself. And now, lo and behold, *the child!* Already he is calling it *the child* when it is no more than a worm in his daughter's womb. What kind of child can seed like that give life to, seed driven into the woman not in love but in hatred, mixed chaotically, meant to soil her, to mark her, like a dog's urine?

A father without the sense to have a son: is this how it is all going to end, is this how his line is going to run out, like water dribbling into the earth? Who would have thought it! A day like any other day, clear skies, a mild sun, yet suddenly everything is changed, utterly changed!

Standing against the wall outside the kitchen, hiding his face in his hands, he heaves and heaves and finally cries.

He installs himself in Lucy's old room, which she has not taken back. For the rest of the afternoon he avoids her, afraid he will come out with something rash.

Over supper there is a new revelation. 'By the way,' she says, 'the boy is back.'

'The boy?'

'Yes, the boy you had the row with at Petrus's party. He is staying with Petrus, helping him. His name is Pollux.'

'Not Mncedisi? Not Nqabayakhe? Nothing unpronounceable, just Pollux?'

'P-O-L-L-U-X. And David, can we have some relief from that terrible irony of yours?'

'I don't know what you mean.'

'Of course you do. For years you used it against me when I was a child, to mortify me. You can't have forgotten. Anyway, Pollux turns out to be a brother of Petrus's wife's. Whether that means a real brother I don't know. But Petrus has obligations toward him, family obligations.'

'So it all begins to come out. And now young Pollux returns to the scene of the crime and we must behave as if nothing has happened.'

'Don't get indignant, David, it doesn't help. According to Petrus, Pollux has dropped out of school and can't find a job. I just want to warn you he is around. I would steer clear of him if I were you. I suspect there is something wrong with him. But I can't order him off the property, it's not in my power.'

'Particularly – ' He does not finish the sentence.

'Particularly what? Say it.'

'Particularly when he may be the father of the child you are carrying. Lucy, your situation is becoming ridiculous, worse than ridiculous, sinister. I don't know how you can fail to see it. I plead with you, leave the farm before it is too late. It's the only sane thing left to do.'

'Stop calling it *the farm*, David. This is not a farm, it's just a piece of land where I grow things – we both know that. But no, I'm not giving it up.'

He goes to bed with a heavy heart. Nothing has changed

between Lucy and himself, nothing has healed. They snap at each other as if he has not been away at all.

It is morning. He clambers over the new-built fence. Petrus's wife is hanging washing behind the old stables. 'Good morning,' he says. '*Molo*. I'm looking for Petrus.'

She does not meet his eyes, but points languidly toward the building site. Her movements are slow, heavy. Her time is near: even he can see that.

Petrus is glazing windows. There is a long palaver of greetings that ought to be gone through, but he is in no mood for it. 'Lucy tells me the boy is back again,' he says. 'Pollux. The boy who attacked her.'

Petrus scrapes his knife clean, lays it down. 'He is my relative,' he says, rolling the *r*. 'Now I must tell him to go away because of this thing that happened?'

'You told me you did not know him. You lied to me.'

Petrus sets his pipe between his stained teeth and sucks vigorously. Then he removes the pipe and gives a wide smile. 'I lie,' he says. 'I lie to you.' He sucks again. 'For why must I lie to you?'

'Don't ask me, ask yourself, Petrus. Why do you lie?'

The smile has vanished. 'You go away, you come back again – why?' He stares challengingly. 'You have no work here. You come to look after your child. I also look after my child.'

'Your child? Now he is your child, this Pollux?'

'Yes. He is a child. He is my family, my people.'

So that is it. No more lies. *My people*. As naked an answer as he could wish. Well, Lucy is *his people*.

'You say it is bad, what happened,' Petrus continues. 'I also say it is bad. It is bad. But it is finish.' He takes the pipe from his mouth, stabs the air vehemently with the stem. 'It is finish.'

'It is not finished. Don't pretend you don't know what I mean. It is not finished. On the contrary, it is just beginning. It will go on long after I am dead and you are dead.'

Petrus stares reflectively, not pretending he does not understand. 'He will marry her,' he says at last. 'He will marry Lucy, only he is too young, too young to be marry. He is a child still.'

'A dangerous child. A young thug. A jackal boy.'

Petrus brushes aside the insults. 'Yes, he is too young, too young. Maybe one day he can marry, but not now. I will marry.'

'You will marry whom?'

'I will marry Lucy.'

He cannot believe his ears. So this is it, that is what all the shadow-boxing was for: this bid, this blow! And here stands Petrus foursquare, puffing on the empty pipe, waiting for a response.

'You will marry Lucy,' he says carefully. 'Explain to me what you mean. No, wait, rather don't explain. This is not something I want to hear. This is not how we do things.'

We: he is on the point of saying, *We Westerners*.

'Yes, I can see, I can see,' says Petrus. He is positively chuckling. 'But I tell you, then you tell Lucy. Then it is over, all this badness.'

'Lucy does not want to marry. Does not want to marry a man. It is not an option she will consider. I can't make myself clearer than that. She wants to live her own life.'

'Yes, I know,' says Petrus. And perhaps he does indeed know. He would be a fool to underestimate Petrus. 'But here', says Petrus, 'it is dangerous, too dangerous. A woman must be marry.'

'I tried to handle it lightly,' he tells Lucy afterwards. 'Though I could hardly believe what I was hearing. It was blackmail pure and simple.'

'It wasn't blackmail. You are wrong about that. I hope you didn't lose your temper.'

'No, I didn't lose my temper. I said I would relay his offer, that's all. I said I doubted you would be interested.'

'Were you offended?'

'Offended at the prospect of becoming Petrus's father-in-law? No. I was taken aback, astonished, dumbfounded, but no, not offended, give me credit for that.'

'Because, I must tell you, this is not the first time. Petrus has been dropping hints for a while now. That I would find it altogether safer to become part of his establishment. It is not a joke, not a threat. At some level he is serious.'

'I have no doubt that in some sense he is serious. The question is, in what sense? Is he aware that you are . . . ?'

'You mean, is he aware of my condition? I have not told him. But I am sure his wife and he will have put two and two together.'

'And that won't make him change his mind?'

'Why should it? It will make me all the more part of the family. In any event, it is not me he is after, he is after the farm. The farm is my dowry.'

'But this is preposterous, Lucy! He is already married! In fact, you told me there are two wives. How can you even contemplate it?'

'I don't believe you get the point, David. Petrus is not offering me a church wedding followed by a honeymoon on the Wild Coast. He is offering an alliance, a deal. I contribute the land, in return for which I am allowed to creep in under his wing. Otherwise, he wants to remind me, I am without protection, I am fair game.'

'And that isn't blackmail? What about the personal side? Is there no personal side to the offer?'

'Do you mean, would Petrus expect me to sleep with him? I'm not sure that Petrus would want to sleep with me, except to drive home his message. But, to be frank, no, I don't want to sleep with Petrus. Definitely not.'

'Then we need not discuss it any further. Shall I convey your decision to Petrus – that his offer is not accepted, and I won't say why?'

'No. Wait. Before you get on your high horse with Petrus, take a moment to consider my situation objectively. Objectively I am a woman alone. I have no brothers. I have a father, but he is far away and anyhow powerless in the terms that matter here. To whom can I turn for protection, for patronage? To Ettinger? It is just a matter of time before Ettinger is found with a bullet in his back. Practically speaking, there is only Petrus left. Petrus may not be a big man but he is big enough for someone small like me. And at least I know Petrus. I have no illusions about him. I know what I would be letting myself in for.'

'Lucy, I am in the process of selling the house in Cape Town. I am prepared to send you to Holland. Alternatively I am prepared to give you whatever you need to set yourself up again somewhere safer than here. Think about it.'

It is as if she has not heard him. 'Go back to Petrus,' she says. 'Propose the following. Say I accept his protection. Say he can put out whatever story he likes about our relationship and I won't contradict him. If he wants me to be known as his third wife, so be it. As his concubine, ditto. But then the child becomes his too. The child becomes part of his family. As for the land, say I will sign the land over to him as long as the house remains mine. I will become a tenant on his land.'

'A *bywoner*.'

'A *bywoner*. But the house remains mine, I repeat that. No one enters this house without my permission. Including him. And I keep the kennels.'

'It's not workable, Lucy. Legally it's not workable. You know that.'

'Then what do you propose?'

She sits in her housecoat and slippers with yesterday's newspaper on her lap. Her hair hangs lank; she is overweight in a slack, unhealthy way. More and more she has begun to look like one of those women who shuffle around the corridors of nursing homes whispering to themselves. Why should Petrus bother to negotiate? She cannot last: leave her alone and in due course she will fall like rotten fruit.

'I have made my proposal. Two proposals.'

'No, I'm not leaving. Go to Petrus and tell him what I have said. Tell him I give up the land. Tell him that he can have it, title deed and all. He will love that.'

There is a pause between them.

'How humiliating,' he says finally. 'Such high hopes, and to end like this.'

'Yes, I agree, it is humiliating. But perhaps that is a good point to start from again. Perhaps that is what I must learn to accept. To start at ground level. With nothing. Not with nothing but. With nothing. No cards, no weapons, no property, no rights, no dignity.'

'Like a dog.'

'Yes, like a dog.'

TWENTY-THREE

IT IS MID-MORNING. He has been out, taking the bulldog Katy for a walk. Surprisingly, Katy has kept up with him, either because he is slower than before or because she is faster. She snuffles and pants as much as ever, but this no longer seems to irritate him.

As they approach the house he notices the boy, the one whom Petrus called *my people*, standing with his face to the back wall. At first he thinks he is urinating; then he realizes he is peering in through the bathroom window, peeping at Lucy.

Katy has begun to growl, but the boy is too absorbed to pay heed. By the time he turns they are upon him. The flat of his hand catches the boy in the face. *'You swine!'* he shouts, and strikes him a second time, so that he staggers. *'You filthy swine!'*

More startled than hurt, the boy tries to run, but trips over his own feet. At once the dog is upon him. Her teeth close over his elbow; she braces her forelegs and tugs, growling. With a shout of pain he tries to pull free. He strikes out with a fist, but his blows lack force and the dog ignores them.

The word still rings in the air: *Swine!* Never has he felt such elemental rage. He would like to give the boy what he deserves: a sound thrashing. Phrases that all his life he has avoided seem suddenly just and right: *Teach him a lesson, Show him his place*. So this is what it is like, he thinks! This is what it is like to be a savage!

He gives the boy a good, solid kick, so that he sprawls sideways. Pollux! What a name!

The dog changes position, mounting the boy's body, tugging grimly at his arm, ripping his shirt. The boy tries to push her off, but she does not budge. 'Ya ya ya ya ya!' he shouts in pain. 'I will kill you!' he shouts.

Then Lucy is on the scene. 'Katy!' she commands.

The dog gives her a sidelong glance but does not obey.

Falling to her knees, Lucy grips the dog's collar, speaking softly and urgently. Reluctantly the dog releases her grip.

'Are you all right?' she says.

The boy is moaning with pain. Snot is running from his nostrils. 'I will kill you!' he heaves. He seems on the point of crying.

Lucy folds back his sleeve. There are score-marks from the dog's fangs; as they watch, pearls of blood emerge on the dark skin.

'Come, let us go and wash it,' she says. The boy sucks in the snot and tears, shakes his head.

Lucy is wearing only a wrapper. As she rises, the sash slips loose and her breasts are bared.

The last time he saw his daughter's breasts they were the demure rosebuds of a six-year-old. Now they are heavy, rounded, almost milky. A stillness falls. He is staring; the boy is staring too, unashamedly. Rage wells up in him again, clouding his eyes.

Lucy turns away from the two of them, covers herself. In a single quick movement the boy scrambles to his feet and dodges out of range. 'We will kill you all!' he shouts. He turns; deliberately trampling the potato bed, he ducks under the wire fence and retreats toward Petrus's house. His gait is cocky once more, though he still nurses his arm.

Lucy is right. Something is wrong with him, wrong in his head. A violent child in the body of a young man. But there is more, some angle to the business he does not understand. What is Lucy up to, protecting the boy?

Lucy speaks. 'This can't go on, David. I can cope with Petrus and his *aanhangers*, I can cope with you, but I can't cope with all of you together.'

'He was staring at you through the window. Are you aware of that?'

'He is disturbed. A disturbed child.'

'Is that an excuse? An excuse for what he did to you?'

Lucy's lips move, but he cannot hear what she says.

'I don't trust him,' he goes on. 'He is shifty. He is like a jackal sniffing around, looking for mischief. In the old days we had a word for people like him. Deficient. Mentally deficient. Morally deficient. He should be in an institution.'

'That is reckless talk, David. If you want to think like that, please keep it to yourself. Anyway, what you think of him is beside the point. He is here, he won't disappear in a puff of smoke, he is a fact of life.' She faces him squarely, squinting into the sunlight. Katy slumps down at her feet, panting lightly, pleased with herself, with her achievements. 'David, we can't go on like this. Everything had settled down, everything was peaceful again, until you came back. I must have peace around me. I am prepared to do anything, make any sacrifice, for the sake of peace.'

'And I am part of what you are prepared to sacrifice?'

She shrugs. 'I didn't say it, you said it.'

'Then I'll pack my bags.'

Hours after the incident his hand still tingles from the blows. When he thinks of the boy and his threats, he seethes with anger. At the same time, he is ashamed of himself. He condemns himself absolutely. He has taught no one a lesson – certainly not the boy. All he has done is to estrange himself further from Lucy. He has shown himself to her in the throes of passion, and clearly she does not like what she sees.

He ought to apologize. But he cannot. He is not, it would seem, in control of himself. Something about Pollux sends him into a rage: his ugly, opaque little eyes, his insolence, but also the thought that like a weed he has been allowed to tangle his roots with Lucy and Lucy's existence.

If Pollux insults his daughter again, he will strike him again. *Du musst dein Leben ändern!*: you must change your life. Well, he is too old to heed, too old to change. Lucy may be able to bend to the tempest; he cannot, not with honour.

That is why he must listen to Teresa. Teresa may be the last one left who can save him. Teresa is past honour. She pushes out her breasts to the sun; she plays the banjo in front of the servants and does not care if they smirk. She has immortal longings, and sings her longings. She will not be dead.

He arrives at the clinic just as Bev Shaw is leaving. They embrace, tentative as strangers. Hard to believe they once lay naked in each other's arms.

'Is this just a visit or are you back for a while?' she asks.

'I am back for as long as is necessary. But I won't be staying with Lucy. She and I aren't hitting it off. I am going to find a room for myself in town.'

'I'm sorry. What is the problem?'

'Between Lucy and myself? Nothing, I hope. Nothing that can't be fixed. The problem is with the people she lives among. When I am added in, we become too many. Too many in too small a space. Like spiders in a bottle.'

An image comes to him from the *Inferno*: the great marsh of Styx, with souls boiling up in it like mushrooms. *Vedi l'anime di color cui vinse l'ira*. Souls overcome with anger, gnawing at each other. A punishment fitted to the crime.

'You are talking about that boy who has moved in with Petrus. I must say I don't like the look of him. But as long as Petrus is there, surely Lucy will be all right. Perhaps the time has come, David, for you to stand back and let Lucy work out solutions for herself. Women are adaptable. Lucy is adaptable. And she is young. She lives closer to the ground than you. Than either of us.'

Lucy adaptable? That is not his experience. 'You keep telling me to stand back,' he says. 'If I had stood back from the beginning, where would Lucy be now?'

Bev Shaw is silent. Is there something about him that Bev Shaw can see and he cannot? Because animals trust her, should he trust her too, to teach him a lesson? Animals trust her, and she uses that trust to liquidate them. What is the lesson there?

'If I were to stand back,' he stumbles on, 'and some new disaster were to take place on the farm, how would I be able to live with myself?'

She shrugs. 'Is that the question, David?' she asks quietly.

'I don't know. I don't know what the question is any more. Between Lucy's generation and mine a curtain seems to have fallen. I didn't even notice when it fell.'

There is a long silence between them.

'Anyway,' he continues, 'I can't stay with Lucy, so I am looking for a room. If you happen to hear of anything in Grahamstown, let me know. What I mainly came to say is that I am available to help at the clinic.'

'That will be handy,' says Bev Shaw.

From a friend of Bill Shaw's he buys a half-ton pickup, for which he pays with a cheque for R1000 and another cheque for R7000 postdated to the end of the month.

'What do you plan to use it for?' says the man.

'Animals. Dogs.'

'You will need rails on the back, so that they won't jump out. I know someone who can fit rails for you.'

'My dogs don't jump.'

According to its papers the truck is twelve years old, but the engine sounds smooth enough. And anyway, he tells himself, it does not have to last for ever. Nothing has to last for ever.

Following up an advertisement in *Grocott's Mail*, he hires a room in a house near the hospital. He gives his name as Lourie, pays a month's rent in advance, tells his landlady he is in Grahamstown for outpatient treatment. He does not say what the treatment is for, but knows she thinks it is cancer.

He is spending money like water. No matter.

At a camping shop he buys an immersion heater, a small gas stove, an aluminium pot. Carrying them up to his room, he meets his landlady on the stairs. 'We don't allow cooking in the rooms, Mr Lourie,' she says. 'In case of fire, you know.'

The room is dark, stuffy, overfurnished, the mattress lumpy. But he will get used to it, as he has got used to other things.

There is one other boarder, a retired schoolteacher. They exchange greetings over breakfast, for the rest do not speak. After breakfast he leaves for the clinic and spends the day there, every day, Sundays included.

The clinic, more than the boarding-house, becomes his home. In the bare compound behind the building he makes a nest of sorts, with a table and an old armchair from the Shaws and a beach umbrella to keep off the worst of the sun. He brings in the gas stove to make tea or warm up canned food: spaghetti and meatballs, snoek and onions. Twice a day he feeds the animals; he cleans out their pens and occasionally talks to them; otherwise he reads or dozes or, when he has the premises to himself, picks out on Lucy's banjo the music he will give to Teresa Guiccioli.

Until the child is born, this will be his life.

One morning he glances up to see the faces of three little boys peering at him over the concrete wall. He rises from his seat; the dogs start barking; the boys drop down and scamper off whooping with excitement. What a tale to tell back home: a mad old man who sits among the dogs singing to himself!

Mad indeed. How can he ever explain, to them, to their parents, to D Village, what Teresa and her lover have done to deserve being brought back to this world?

TWENTY-FOUR

IN HER WHITE nightdress Teresa stands at the bedroom window. Her eyes are closed. It is the darkest hour of the night: she breathes deeply, breathing in the rustle of the wind, the belling of the bullfrogs.

'*Che vuol dir,*' she sings, her voice barely above a whisper – '*Che vuol dir questa solitudine immensa? Ed io,*' she sings – '*che sono?*'

Silence. The *solitudine immensa* offers no reply. Even the trio in the corner are quiet as dormice.

'Come!' she whispers. 'Come to me, I plead, my Byron!' She opens her arms wide, embracing the darkness, embracing what it will bring.

She wants him to come on the wind, to wrap himself around her, to bury his face in the hollow between her breasts. Alternatively she wants him to arrive on the dawn, to appear on the horizon as a sun-god casting the glow of his warmth upon her. By any means at all she wants him back.

Sitting at his table in the dog-yard, he harkens to the sad, swooping curve of Teresa's plea as she confronts the darkness. This is a bad time of the month for Teresa, she is sore, she has not slept a wink, she is haggard with longing. She wants to be rescued – from the pain, from the summer heat, from the Villa Gamba, from her father's bad temper, from everything.

From the chair where it rests she picks up the mandolin. Cradling it like a child, she returns to the window. *Plink-plunk* goes the mandolin in her arms, softly, so as not to wake her father. *Plink-plunk* squawks the banjo in the desolate yard in Africa.

Just something to dabble at, he had said to Rosalind. A lie. The opera is not a hobby, not any more. It consumes him night and day.

Yet despite occasional good moments, the truth is that *Byron in Italy* is going nowhere. There is no action, no development, just a long, halting cantilena hurled by Teresa into the empty air, punctuated now and then with groans and sighs from Byron offstage. The husband and the rival mistress are forgotten, might as well not exist. The lyric impulse in him may not be dead, but after decades of starvation it can crawl forth from its cave only pinched, stunted, deformed. He has not the musical resources, the resources of energy, to raise *Byron in Italy* off the monotonous track on which it has been running since the start. It has become the kind of work a sleepwalker might write.

He sighs. It would have been nice to be returned triumphant to society as the author of an eccentric little chamber opera. But that will not be. His hopes must be more temperate: that somewhere from amidst the welter of sound there will dart up, like a bird, a single authentic note of immortal longing. As for recognizing it, he will leave that to the scholars of the future, if there are still scholars by then. For he will not hear the note himself, when it comes, if it comes – he knows too much about art and the ways of art to expect that. Though it would have been nice for Lucy to hear proof in her lifetime, and think a little better of him.

Poor Teresa! Poor aching girl! He has brought her back from the grave, promised her another life, and now he is failing her. He hopes she will find it in her heart to forgive him.

Of the dogs in the holding pens, there is one he has come to feel a particular fondness for. It is a young male with a withered left hindquarter which it drags behind it. Whether it was born like that he does not know. No visitor has shown an interest in adopting it. Its period of grace is almost over; soon it will have to submit to the needle.

Sometimes, while he is reading or writing, he releases it from the pen and lets it frisk, in its grotesque way, around the yard, or snooze at his feet. It is not 'his' in any sense; he has been careful not to give it a name (though Bev Shaw refers to it as *Driepoot*); nevertheless, he is sensible of a generous affection streaming out toward him from the dog. Arbitrarily, unconditionally, he has been adopted; the dog would die for him, he knows.

The dog is fascinated by the sound of the banjo. When he strums the strings, the dog sits up, cocks its head, listens. When he hums Teresa's line, and the humming begins to swell with feeling (it is as though his larynx thickens: he can feel the hammer of blood in his throat), the dog smacks its lips and seems on the point of singing too, or howling.

Would he dare to do that: bring a dog into the piece, allow it to loose its own lament to the heavens between the strophes of lovelorn Teresa's? Why not? Surely, in a work that will never be performed, all things are permitted?

On Saturday mornings, by agreement, he goes to Donkin Square to help Lucy at the market stall. Afterwards he takes her out to lunch.

Lucy is slowing down in her movements. She has begun to wear a self-absorbed, placid look. She is not obviously pregnant; but if he is picking up signs, how much longer before the eagle-eyed daughters of Grahamstown pick them up too?

'How is Petrus getting on?' he asks.

'The house is finished, all but the ceilings and the plumbing. They are in the process of moving in.'

'And their child? Isn't the child just about due?'

'Next week. All very nicely timed.'

'Has Petrus dropped any more hints?'

'Hints?'

'About you. About your place in the scheme.'

'No.'

'Perhaps it will be different once the child' – he makes the faintest of gestures toward his daughter, toward her body – 'is born. It will be, after all, a child of this earth. They will not be able to deny that.'

There is a long silence between them.

'Do you love him yet?'

Though the words are his, from his mouth, they startle him.

'The child? No. How could I? But I will. Love will grow – one can trust Mother Nature for that. I am determined to be a good mother, David. A good mother and a good person. You should try to be a good person too.'

'I suspect it is too late for me. I'm just an old lag serving out my sentence. But you go ahead. You are well on the way.'

A good person. Not a bad resolution to make, in dark times.

By unspoken agreement, he does not, for the time being, come to his daughter's farm. Nonetheless, one weekday he takes a drive along the Kenton road, leaves the truck at the turnoff, and walks the rest of the way, not following the track but striking out over the veld.

From the last hillcrest the farm opens out before him: the old house, solid as ever, the stables, Petrus's new house, the old dam on which he can make out specks that must be the ducks and larger specks that must be the wild geese, Lucy's visitors from afar.

At this distance the flowerbeds are solid blocks of colour: magenta, carnelian, ash-blue. A season of blooming. The bees must be in their seventh heaven.

Of Petrus there is no sign, nor of his wife or the jackal boy who runs with them. But Lucy is at work among the flowers; and, as he picks his way down the hillside, he can see the bulldog too, a patch of fawn on the path beside her.

He reaches the fence and stops. Lucy, with her back to him, has not yet noticed him. She is wearing a pale summer dress, boots, and a wide straw hat. As she bends over, clipping or pruning or tying, he can see the milky, blue-veined skin and broad, vulnerable tendons of the backs of her knees: the least beautiful part of a woman's body, the least expressive, and therefore perhaps the most endearing.

Lucy straightens up, stretches, bends down again. Field-labour; peasant tasks, immemorial. His daughter is becoming a peasant.

Still she is not aware of him. As for the watchdog, the watchdog appears to be snoozing.

So: once she was only a little tadpole in her mother's body, and now here she is, solid in her existence, more solid than he has ever been. With luck she will last a long time, long beyond him. When he is dead she will, with luck, still be here doing her ordinary tasks among the flowerbeds. And from within her will have issued another existence, that with luck will be just as solid, just as long-lasting. So it will go on, a line of existences in which his share, his gift, will grow inexorably less and less, till it may as well be forgotten.

A grandfather. A Joseph. Who would have thought it! What pretty girl can he expect to be wooed into bed with a grandfather?

Softly he speaks her name. 'Lucy!'

She does not hear him.

What will it entail, being a grandfather? As a father he has not been much of a success, despite trying harder than most. As a grandfather he will probably score lower than average too. He lacks the virtues of the old: equanimity, kindliness, patience. But perhaps those virtues will come as other virtues go: the virtue of passion, for instance. He must have a look again at Victor Hugo, poet of grandfatherhood. There may be things to learn.

The wind drops. There is a moment of utter stillness which he would wish prolonged for ever: the gentle sun, the stillness of mid-afternoon, bees busy in a field of flowers; and at the centre of the picture a young woman, *das ewig Weibliche*, lightly pregnant, in a straw sunhat. A scene ready-made for a Sargent or a Bonnard. City boys like him; but even city boys can recognize beauty when they see it, can have their breath taken away.

The truth is, he has never had much of an eye for rural life, despite all his reading in Wordsworth. Not much of an eye for anything, except pretty girls; and where has that got him? Is it too late to educate the eye?

He clears his throat. 'Lucy,' he says, more loudly.

The spell is broken. Lucy comes erect, half-turns, smiles. 'Hello,' she says. 'I didn't hear you.'

Katy raises her head and stares shortsightedly in his direction.

He clambers through the fence. Katy lumbers up to him, sniffs his shoes.

'Where is the truck?' asks Lucy. She is flushed from her labours and perhaps a little sunburnt. She looks, suddenly, the picture of health.

'I parked and took a walk.'

'Will you come in and have some tea?'

She makes the offer as if he were a visitor. Good. Visitorship, visitation: a new footing, a new start.

Sunday has come again. He and Bev Shaw are engaged in one of their sessions of *Lösung*. One by one he brings in the cats, then the dogs: the old, the blind, the halt, the crippled, the maimed, but also the young, the sound – all those whose term has come. One by one Bev touches them, speaks to them, comforts them, and puts them away, then stands back and watches while he seals up the remains in a black plastic shroud.

He and Bev do not speak. He has learned by now, from her, to concentrate all his attention on the animal they are killing, giving it what he no longer has difficulty in calling by its proper name: love.

He ties the last bag and takes it to the door. Twenty-three. There is only the young dog left, the one who likes music, the one who, given half a chance, would already have lolloped after his comrades into the clinic building, into the theatre with its zinc-topped table where the rich, mixed smells still linger, including one he will not yet have met with in his life: the smell of expiration, the soft, short smell of the released soul.

What the dog will not be able to work out (*not in a month of Sundays!* he thinks), what his nose will not tell him, is how one can enter what seems to be an ordinary room and never come out again. Something happens in this room, something unmention-able: here the soul is yanked out of the body; briefly it hangs about in the air, twisting and contorting; then it is sucked away and is gone. It will be beyond him, this room that is not a room but a hole where one leaks out of existence.

It gets harder all the time, Bev Shaw once said. Harder, yet easier too. One gets used to things getting harder; one ceases to be surprised that what used to be as hard as hard can be grows harder yet. He can save the young dog, if he wishes, for another week. But a time must come, it cannot be evaded, when he will have to bring him to Bev Shaw in her operating room (perhaps he will carry him in his arms, perhaps he will do that for him) and caress him and brush back the fur so that the needle can find the vein, and whisper to him and support him in the moment when, bewilderingly, his legs buckle; and then, when the soul is out, fold him up and pack him away in his bag, and the next day wheel the bag into the flames and see that it is burnt, burnt up. He will do all that for him when his time comes. It will be little enough, less than little: nothing.

He crosses the surgery. 'Was that the last?' asks Bev Shaw.

'One more.'

He opens the cage door. 'Come,' he says, bends, opens his arms. The dog wags its crippled rear, sniffs his face, licks his cheeks, his lips, his ears. He does nothing to stop it. 'Come.'

Bearing him in his arms like a lamb, he re-enters the surgery. 'I thought you would save him for another week,' says Bev Shaw. 'Are you giving him up?'

'Yes, I am giving him up.'